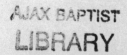

D.J. laughed in spite of himself. Instantly, he wished he hadn't. The mother bear dropped down on all fours and came lumbering toward him. . . . D.J. watched in terror as the sow's hooked, ugly claws inched closer to his feet. He drew back until he was in danger of falling over backward. When the bear's right front claw touched his boot sole, D.J. raised his foot slightly and kicked at the forepaw. At the same time he screeched in panic. . . .

Instantly, the dog rushed in, leaped high and grabbed a mouthful of bear hair. The sow roared, dropped to all fours and thrust out her long neck with her terrible jaws open to crush the mutt. Zero barked and dashed away, but this time the bear was just a half-jump behind.

LEE RODDY is a best-selling author of more than 50 books. He lives in the Sierra Nevada Mountains of California and devotes his time to writing books and public speaking. He is a co-writer of the book which became the TV series, "The Life and Times of Grizzly Adams."

Born on an Illinois farm and reared on a California ranch, Lee Roddy grew up around hunters and trail hounds. As a boy, he began writing animal stories. He spent lots of time reading about dogs, horses, and other animals. These stories shaped his thinking and values before he went to Hollywood to write professionally. His Christian commitment later turned his writing talents to books like this one.

Buck Hudson, a long-time Roddy family friend, is a Christian layman who once hunted bears. He and the author's father, T.L. (Jack) Roddy, shared with the author many memories and details about bears and hounds.

Since this story was written, laws have changed. It is now illegal for hunters to do some of the things described in this book.

The Hair-Pulling Bear Dog

LEE RODDY

VICTOR BOOKS

A DIVISION OF SCRIPTURE PRESS PUBLICATIONS INC.
USA CANADA ENGLAND

THE D.J. DILLON
ADVENTURE SERIES

10 11 12 13 14 15 16 17 18 19 20 Printing/Year 00 99 98 97 96

Scripture quotations are from the *New American Standard Bible,*
© the Lockman Foundation, 1960, 1962, 1963, 1968, 1971, 1972, 1973,
1975, 1977.

Library of Congress Catalog Card Number: 84-52036
ISBN: 1-56476-502-4

CONTENTS

ACKNOWLEDGMENT

There's a secret behind the D.J. Dillon Adventure
Series. It all began when I was 14. I knew then that
someday I wanted to write books like this one. So I
wrote and wrote—for 39 long years—before the first
book sold. I sold other works, but not the 11 books
I'd written. I would probably have given up if it hadn't
been for that secret.

On my first day of college, I met red-haired Cicely
Price. Over the next four years, I often told her that
someday I was going to be an author. She believed
me. She believed me when my other writing sold, even
though my books were rejected by publishers, year
after year.

She believed in me when we were married, for
our first major purchase was a typewriter. Cicely
believed in me when I sat on the edge of our bed and
wrote on a typewriter perched on a chair. She believed
in me when we knelt by our son's crib and thanked

God for our firstborn, and I still hadn't sold a book. Cicely believed in me when our daughter was born three years later, and the publishers' rejections were still coming.

In those long years, I often got discouraged—but Cicely never did. She still believed in me when our children were in college—and I recommitted my life to the Lord. Shortly after that, in November of 1974, my first book sold.

Since 1974, I've written or coauthored more than 40 books. Not one of them would ever have been written if it hadn't been for the secret staying power of my wife's encouragement and faith.

There is no way I can say how much it means to me to have her love, support, and enduring faith for all these years. This acknowledgment is only a small token of how grateful I am to have had Cicely in my life—with her faith.

May God bring someone into your life who believes in you . . . until you can believe in yourself.

LEE RODDY

Chapter One

COMING OF THE OUTLAW BEAR

At first, D.J. Dillon thought the terrible nightmare
had returned. In his sleep, he again heard the squeal of
brakes, the crash, and then the awful silence. The
13-year-old boy's blue eyes blinked open. He stared
into the soft moonlit darkness of the kitchen where
he slept on a rollaway bed.

His blond head turned automatically toward his
parents' bedroom wall beside him. He started to call
softly, "Mom?" Then he remembered.

She was dead six months now, killed in that auto
accident. The mountain's silence had carried the
sound for miles. D.J. had heard it up the canyon
without knowing who was in the collision.

Memories flashed over him again. The hurt swallowed him like a silent, ugly monster. D.J. started to
turn over and bury his face in the dusty pillow when
he heard the crash again—but now he was wide
awake!

He jumped out of bed. His bare feet hit the faded linoleum. "Dad! Grandpa! The pigs! Something's after the pigs!"

In his shorts, D.J. ran past the wood-burning cookstove, past the sink, and to the back door. He jerked it open and dashed into the warm June night without even picking up a flashlight. The full moon outlined the Sierra Nevada Mountains, the evergreen trees, and the sagging outbuildings. The boy ran bare-footed toward the small lean-to where Grandpa Dillon's shoats* were penned. D.J. thought, *Probably some dumb ol' dog!*

Grandpa Dillon always said D.J. was half boy and half jackrabbit because of the way he ran. Running on his toes, the mountain boy made no more sound than the gentle night breeze. He passed Grandpa's vegetable and rose garden with the single strand of electric fence to keep the deer out.

D.J. slowed only enough to pick up a couple of hard dirt clods. Then he raced on, out of the moonlight into the deep shadows of the old shed. D.J. drew his arm back, ready to throw the dirt clod when he rounded the corner where the pigpen was.

He stopped instantly. So did his heart. There, clearly visible in the full moon, was a wild bear!

He stood on his hind legs like a man, but this bear seemed as tall as the ponderosas* growing on the mountainsides. His eyes glowed orange in the moonlight. D.J. could see the bear was night-black except for a white blaze on his chest. A limp, freshly-killed

*You can find an explanation of the starred words under "Life in Stoney Ridge" on pages 138-141.

shoat lay in the bear's great, shaggy arms.

D.J.'s brain screamed, *Run! Run!* but his legs weren't listening. D.J. could only stare at the bear and the dead weaning pig. It looked small as a kitten in those ugly, hooked claws the size of D.J.'s head. Goosebumps chased themselves up and down the boy's bare arms and across his shoulders.

The bear made a warning "whoof" sound and clicked his teeth. He huffed again, dropped the pig, and came down on all four feet. D.J. dropped the dirt clods as the bear charged. D.J.'s legs came to life and he spun around. But in that moment he saw the animal's lower jaw was swollen and deformed. The jackrabbit in D.J. took over and he ran in great, leaping bounds back toward the house.

"Bear!" The word came out weak and croaky. D.J. tried again, louder. "Bear! Dad! Grandpa! A bear!" This time, D.J.'s voice worked fine. The hundred people living in Stoney Ridge 10 miles away might have heard him. D.J. ran like a scalded cat around the shed. He almost ran into his father racing toward the boy from the house. Sam Dillon carried his old Krag* rifle and a five-celled flashlight.

D.J. yelled, "Look out, Dad! Killer bear!" The boy pointed wildly in the direction of the pigpen and fell in behind his father. He stepped wide around the corner and threw up the light and gun.

D.J. yelled, "There he goes!"

The bear was hightailing for tall timber. It was amazing how fast such a big, clumsy-looking monster could move. He was bounding in a rolling gait through the downed hog-wire fence and toward the safety of California's Sierra Nevada Mountains.

D.J.'s father fired the long-barreled .30-.40 caliber rifle. The explosion almost broke D.J.'s eardrums. But in the flashlight's bobbing beam, D.J. saw the bear was still running. The boy heard his father frantically working the bolt to put another shell under the firing pin. Before he could again raise the weapon, the bear topped a ravine of pines and cedars and disappeared.

From that moment on, D.J. Dillon's life was forever changed.

An hour later, sitting on homemade benches at the living room table, D.J.'s father still was "cussing a blue streak," as D.J.'s mom used to say. Sam Dillon was a powerfully built man with a huge chest that seemed out of proportion to his short legs. He sat in his old frayed blue pajama bottoms. He repeatedly pounded his powerful right fist into his open left palm. D.J. saw the callouses that had formed even through heavy gloves from his dad's work as a choke-setter* in the timber.

Dad said again, "No doubt about it! This here's the outlaw bear we been hearing about! The bee men and the livestock ranchers got a big reward on his ornery hide! But this is the first time he's ever struck on this side of Stoney Ridge."

D.J. felt weak and all talked out from telling his story many times to Grandpa Dillon. He was a feisty little man with a contrary streak as wide as a barn door. Grandpa was thin as a piece of baling wire, but he was slightly stooped. He was still excited, waving what he called his Irish shillelagh,* a blackthorn cane he used because of an arthritic hip.

Grandpa wore his long johns, as he always did,

even in spring and summer. His small, round wire-rimmed bifocals rested far down on his thin nose. Without his teeth, his mouth looked funny.

"Did you see that bear's footprint, D.J.?" Grandpa asked for the umpteenth time. D.J. nodded. He had seen the track clearly when Dad turned his flashlight on the smelly, soft earth of the pigpen. But Grandpa didn't wait for a reply. He slapped the shillelagh on the oilcloth so hard the heavy coffee mugs jumped. "A splayfoot, that's what it was, D.J.! The left hind foot was sorta broad and flat and turned outward. Deformed, maybe from being caught in a trap, or injured or something."

D.J. looked around the room, hardly seeing the bare electric light bulb swinging by its long cord above them. He didn't see the familiar wallpaper that peeled and curled. There were some old pictures that had been his mother's, and a picture of Jesus saved from a calendar. The wood-burning heating stove sat toward the kitchen. Dad's bedroom door opened right behind the stove. Dad's and Grandpa's rooms were separated by an incompleted bathroom. It held only a tub and a homemade closet. The other facilities were outside in back of the house. Besides the table and benches, the only other piece of furniture in the living room was a broken-down horsehair sofa placed just under the side window. Behind the sofa was Dad's five-string banjo, Grandpa's fiddle in a dusty black case, and a guitar that had belonged to D.J.'s mom. None of the instruments had been touched in months.

D.J. loved Grandpa in a special way, though Mom used to say he was "quite a character." D.J. long ago had realized Grandpa saw things in different ways from most people. Instead of being mad like his son over the outlaw bear's raid, Grandpa cackled like a Rhode Island Red hen. "That bear must weigh 3 or 400 pounds. And he's got a regular suitcase of a foot! A real satchel foot! That's what I'll call him: Ol' Satchel Foot!"

Grandpa liked to name things. No matter what an animal's name was, Grandpa gave it another. That was one of the reasons he and his son argued so much. Each man said the other was contrary.

Suddenly, Dad slammed his powerful hand down on the rickety table so hard D.J. jumped. Dad cried, "I got it!" He scratched his two-day old growth of fierce black whiskers. "We'll get us a dog! I'll go back to bear hunting like I used to before D.J. was born!"

D.J.'s heart jumped so high it nearly sailed out of his mouth. "A dog, Dad? *Really?* Just before school let out, I heard about a kid who had collie pups for sale."

"Collie?" Dad's voice cracked like a rifle shot. He had a hair-trigger temper and he was still mad about the outlaw bear killing the pig. Dad's sun-browned face went black, right down to his thick neck and powerful shoulders. "Don't you go bringing that idee up again, David Jonathan Dillon!"

Grandpa wasn't nearly so powerfully built as his son, but he was every bit as bullheaded under that thin, white hair. "Now, Sam, the boy has been wanting that there kind of dog for quite a spell, and—"

Dad interrupted with a roar. "No pretty dogs! What we need is a bear dog! A genuine hound dog!" Dad jumped up from the splintery bench and began pacing. "We can use the bounty money!"

D.J. felt his stomach twist and fall right down to his ankles. For as long as he could remember, he'd wanted a collie. With a collie, D.J. wouldn't be so lonely. He'd have a friend to talk to in the summertime and to roam the woods with.

But Dad was as strong in his opinions as in his body. In fact, Dad was about the strongest man D.J.'d ever seen. D.J. was just exactly the opposite: tall for his age, skinny, fair, and freckled with uncombed pale yellowish-white hair spilling over his forehead. Grandpa always claimed D.J. took after his mother's side of the family.

Dad turned to glare at his father. "Maybe two or three hounds." Dad seemed to be daring Grandpa to say something against that idea.

D.J. saw the "pure cussedness," as his mom used to say, raise up in Grandpa's pale blue eyes. D.J. was sure the two men were going to get into another argument. But Grandpa didn't say anything. Maybe that was because D.J.'s eyes were begging Grandpa not to argue anymore. When Mom was alive, she kept the two men peaceable most of the time. But D.J. couldn't do that.

Dad said, "Yessiree, D.J.! Trail hounds! Bear hounds!" His bare feet made little dusty puffs from the splintery pine floor. "Real hounds that'll run down varmints and help set meat on the table. And that reward is waiting for me! All I got to do is take it out of that bear's ornery hide! Those hounds'll guarantee we get that bounty!"

Grandpa asked, "Sam, where you going to get any hounds around here?"

Dad slapped his strong hands together with satisfaction. "I'll go trade with Boot Malloy first thing tomorrow! Then I'll get after that bear!"

Grandpa snorted. "Malloy will skin you alive and
make you thank him for doing it!"

"He won't, neither! You're just talking through
your hat again!"

The argument was on. The boy jumped up and
ran out the front screen door which opened onto an
unscreened L-shaped porch. The porch stood on
posts about three feet off the ground in front of the
house and about a foot off the ground on the side behind the sofa. Grandpa's red cane-bottom rocking
chair was just outside the door. D.J. ignored it. He
sat down on the top step and looked through the evergreen conifers* toward the county road.

The Dillon's small frame house, once yellow but
long unpainted, was the only dwelling for two miles.
The rented house stood alone atop a small hill a
good quarter-mile back in the ponderosas and cedars.
There wasn't even a dirt driveway from the paved
county road. D.J. heard the crickets in their nightly
chorus. A big old bullfrog sang *chug-a-rum, chug-a-
rum* in a deep bass voice from the pond down by the
creek.

D.J. usually enjoyed the mountain sounds. But tonight he hurt too much. He looked up at the Milky Way
and all the millions of stars and whispered fiercely,
"I don't want a hound! I want a collie!"

His mother had sided with him in favor of the collie, but it hadn't done any good. Usually, Grandpa
spoke up for D.J. The old man seemed to understand
a boy without friends his own age needed a dog

for a companion. That was especially true during
school vacations.

D.J. had told Grandpa his reason for wanting the
dog. "If I had a collie, we could have adventures
together and I could write stories about him." D.J.
had always loved to read. He had made up his mind
that someday he'd be a famous author of dog stories.

D.J. also wanted a boy his own age for a friend.
D.J. wanted Dad and Grandpa to quit arguing all the
time. Grandpa had once said, "D.J., you got a powerful lot of wants for one boy."

But mostly D.J. wanted a collie to be with him—to
play with and just to have someone to talk to who
didn't always argue. Not one kid anywhere near his
own age lived closer than a couple of miles. Since
school had let out two weeks before, not a single
person had waded across the creek and climbed the
red dust road to the Dillon house.

The mountain boy raised his eyes to the night
skies again. He hadn't prayed since his mother died because he wasn't really sure God was real or answered prayer. But the boy was hurting enough that
his lips moved.

"Why?" he whispered. "Why can't I have a collie?
I got nothing else. Is that too much to ask?"

There was no answer, just the light spring breeze
whispering in the ponderosas and cedars, the crickets
in the dry grass, and the deep, booming voice of the
big old bullfrog in the distance.

D.J. leaned against the rough porch wall and
closed his eyes against the world. He sat there a long-
time, hearing Dad and Grandpa argue, and "hurting
all over more than anyplace else," as Grandpa would

say.

And D.J. knew it was going to get worse because of that bear.

Chapter Two

THE HAIR-PULLER'S SECRET

Things got worse the next afternoon when D.J. rode in his dad's old blue pickup truck toward Boot Malloy's place. Sam Dillon had gone about a mile up a winding, narrow dirt road when he rounded a curve and started across a sagging wooden bridge. At the same time, a big black pickup swung around a pile of boulders from the other direction. The other driver kept coming, honking angrily. Dad slammed on the brakes so hard that D.J.'s head snapped forward. Only then did the other driver stop.

Dad yelled out of the open window. "Don't you know nothing 'bout mountain driving, Mister?"

The other driver was a big man with unshaven heavy jaws. "I'm in a hurry! Back up and let me through!"

Dad's hair-trigger temper went off. He leaped from the pickup and almost ran across the bridge. D.J. started after him. Both doors on the black pickup opened. The big driver jumped out and his passenger trailed him. D.J. stopped, not recognizing either person.

The passenger was a boy who looked like he had just swallowed a gallon of vinegar. He wore dirty bib overalls over his sturdy body. His face was like a weasel's—narrow and thin with bright, mean eyes. D.J. figured him to be about 14 and full of fight. The boy made two fists and smiled at D.J. But it was a hard smile. D.J. swallowed hard.

Dad yelled at the big driver, "You want to learn some mountain manners the hard way, Mister?"

The big driver's lips curled in a sneer. "Who's gonna teach me?"

Before Sam Dillon could answer or reach the man, a hound barked from the back of the black pickup. D.J. saw the dog's long, floppy ears and recognized the breed as a black and tan. The dog leaped to the ground and crashed off through the brush.

Both people from the black pickup stopped and looked after the hound. The driver ordered, "Get him, Nails! If he gets away from us again, we'll never catch him."

The boy called Nails ran after the hound. He yelled, "You got to help me, Pop!"

For a moment, the man hesitated. Then he scowled at Sam Dillon, who had stopped at the far side of the little bridge. The man said in a hard tone, "Me'n you'll meet again, Shorty!"

D.J.'s dad yelled, "Don't call me that! I'm Sam Dillon, and I'll whup ye good if you ever cross my path again!"

"I'm Tinsley Abst, and I'll surely give you the plea-

sure to try! My boy'll take care of your kid for no extra charge too!" The man ran after his son.

D.J. sighed with relief. Dad waited until he was
sure Tinsley Abst and Nails weren't coming right back.
Then Dad got in the black pickup and backed it off
the road. D.J. listened to the Absts chasing the hound
while Dad returned to the old blue pickup. D.J. got
back in and they drove on toward Boot Malloy's place.

* * * * *

Sam Dillon squatted on his boot heels and asked
Boot Malloy about the Absts. Malloy was an old bache-
lor with the most innocent-looking brown eyes D.J.
had ever seen outside of Sunday School. Dad had told
D.J. on the drive over that Boot was a snuff-dipping,
slick-tongued horse trader who'd skin you out of your
eyeteeth and then always ask for something "to
boot."

The trader also squatted on his boot heels before
answering. "They're a couple of hard cases. Father and
son. Professional bear hunters. Tinsley Abst told me
he'd come in from over Jawbone Ridge to collect the
bounty on the outlaw bear of Stoney Ridge. He
wanted to trade me that black and tan of his. But I
didn't like the look in that hound's eyes. So, Sam and
D.J., you're getting the pick of my trail hounds."

Dad got up and began checking seven hounds
chained in the shade of Boot Malloy's sagging red
barn. Dad commented on the poor condition of the
hounds' pads, which had been badly cut from running
in rough country. Their hides showed old scars and
some fresh wounds from bear fights.

Boot Malloy wouldn't say who he'd traded with
for the hounds, but said they were real trail hounds

that wouldn't run "trash" like deer, but only varmints like 'coons, mountain lions, and bears. D.J.
thought they were the sorriest looking bunch of hounds
he'd ever seen.

The boy looked around the place where he'd often
come when Dad needed to swap for something. Boot
Malloy had just about everything. Most of it was
junk. D.J. saw rusted logging equipment like the cables
used to "set chokes" and pull logs out of the forest after the trees had been felled. D.J.'s blue eyes took in
some "Swede fiddles," or two-man handsaws. Everything was scattered in the now-drying tall grass.
Stacks of weathered scrap lumber and kegs of rusty
nails were piled by dangerously leaning sheds.

The boy's eyes came back to his father. Dad pointed. "Boot, I'll take those four miserable-looking hounds
off your hands so's you won't have to feed them."

Dad's stubby finger leveled on three hounds—a
black and tan, a mixed redbone and blue tick, and a
mixture of bloodhound,* what Boot called a "Heinz
57 Varieties." Dad hesitated and then added, "And I'll
take that female walker even though she's not much
more than a pup and probably worthless."

D.J. saw Boot Malloy shake his head. "Sam, you
want my four best dogs! That black and tan is ol' Rock,
my best 'cold nose.' He can follow a bear's trail a day
old, even in deep dust. The redbone and blue tick is
called Thunder—a natural born trail hound. That
bloodhound and Heinzhound is Max. He's almost as
good a 'pappy' dog as Rock, only younger. On top of
that, you're a' asking me to give up Roxie who's going
to have her first litter—"

Dad interrupted. "Take it or leave it, Boot."

The trader slowly stood, towering thin as a lodge-
pole pine. He looked down from his 6-foot height
and said, "Guess so, except—like I told you—I can't
sell you my hair-puller.*"

Dad's hair-trigger temper flared. "Don't go trying
to jack up the price on me, Boot Malloy! Let's see that
heeler.*"

D.J. followed the two men inside the barn. The
mountain boy was intrigued, for he'd been around
hunters and dogs all his life, but he'd never heard of
a hair-puller or a heeler before.

D.J. heard a chain rattle. The contrast from the
bright sun to the barn's deep shadows kept the boy
from seeing the dog at first.

Boot said, "Sam, I really want to tell you why you
don't want this here particular dog. He's only about 10
months old, and on his first bear hunt, he—"

Dad interrupted. "I know your tricks, Boot!" Dad
turned toward his son. "D.J., you've been wanting a
dog. I'll just give you this one."

"Ah, Dad, I don't want *him!* I want a collie."

Dad broke in. "What mixture is he, Boot?"

"Oh, about half-hound so he'll hunt. A quarter
Airedale and a quarter Australian shepherd, I'd say.
Shepherds always go for the hind legs, you know.
Natural for a heeler like this one."

D.J. saw the mutt run to the end of his chain. He
was smaller than a hound. The dog stood on his hind
legs supported by his collar. His front legs scratched
the air. The mutt had a long, funny black nose that
stuck out from his muzzle like a plum on a thumb.
He was sort of reddish-brown and shaggy haired with
a stub tail. D.J. decided that this was the world's ug-

liest dog.

Boot said, "Don't be fooled by that hair-puller's powerful good looks, Sam. He's not the dog you want."

D.J. covered his mouth so he could smother a snicker. The dog spotted D.J. and began wiggling in pure joy. The mutt whined and danced on his hind legs, straining against his chain. He was shaking his stub-tailed body as though he'd break in two.

"Look at that, Sam!" Boot cried. "The hair-puller has purely taken to your boy!"

Dad inspected the mutt's pads and felt him all over. "Big scars under his hide," Dad announced with satisfaction. "Still a little tender. Been in a bear fight not long ago, I reckon. Tell you what, Boot. I'll give you a hindquarter of that bear for this hair-puller."

"Now, Sam, I don't want to go demeaning you none, but you ain't got that bear yet."

Dad's contrary streak was showing. "If I don't get that bear, then I'll give you one of my hogs when they're butchered."

"Sam, you don't *want* this here hair-puller!"

"Don't tell me what I want!" Dad snapped. "Deal or not?"

"Sam, I call on your son to witness that I don't want to sell you that there particular dog."

Dad roared, "I won't let you jack up the price a penny more! You wanna deal or not?"

Boot took off his grimy red-billed cap. "Well, Sam, since you're a'forcing me—OK—but what'll you give me to boot?"

*   *   *   *   *

On the bouncy ride back to the paved county road with the four hounds and the dog in the back end, Dad was happy as a bear in a colony of beehives. He was explaining the various terms used for the hounds.

"A 'cold nose' or 'pappy' dog starts a trail. When he gets it running pretty good, you turn in the second one. He'll go to the first dog's baying. After a while, you feed in the third hound that'll follow the first two. You can also let go of the fourth hound at the same time, or you can hold him a little. When they've got the bear lined out and maybe even looking at him, you turn in the fourth dog. That's the hair-puller we got back there.

"But he doesn't necessarily run to join the other dogs. That's why he's sometimes called a 'cut-across' dog or a 'turn-in' dog. Some people call him a 'hair-puller' or 'heeler' or 'catch' dog. You see, D.J., a hair-puller's the best thing a man can have on a bear hunt. Might even save your life, and he's bound to keep your dogs from getting killed. Hounds are necessary to trail and tree a bear. Takes a hound's nose to run a trail. But in the fighting that sometimes follows before the hunter gets there, you need a fast little heeler that has no 'nose,' but runs to the sound of the fight.

"He's strictly a turn-in dog. Sometimes the hair-puller will 'wind' or smell the bear. Then the mutt will cut across, following the bear's scent on the air. This dog might be the first one to hit the bear. By then, the other hounds are probably 'wind running,' their heads thrown up in the air and heading straight for the bear.

"With a hair-puller, they'll usually put a bear up a tree. Maybe the mutt will hang onto a bear's hind leg until he's 10, 12 feet up in the air before the dog lets go. But if a bear's too old or fat or big to climb a tree,

he'll back up against a log or boulder or something
and make a fight of it. That's when you can lose your
hounds if you don't get there soon.

"So you need a heeler like this to keep the hounds
from getting hurt until you get there. You see, a hair-
puller always goes for the bear's backsides, but a
hound tends to go for the front of a bear. Naturally,
that's the most dangerous part. So if it wasn't for the
hair-puller always going for the other end and keeping
the bear off balance, the hounds might all get
killed."

D.J. listened with some interest in spite of his dis-
appointment. His father continued, "A bear has a very
sensitive backside. He can't abide having his 'tail
feathers' pulled. So that's exactly what a hair-puller
does. He's so little and quick that he just keeps getting behind a bear and nipping at his hindquarters
while the hounds worry his head and shoulders."

"Then," D.J. guessed, "when the bear turns on the
hair-puller, the hounds close in again on the bear's
head and sides. The mutt just jumps out of the way
until the bear turns back to deal with the hounds. Then
the hair-puller dashes in again and tries to get a
handful of the bear's hide near his tail. The bear is
fighting on two fronts, and he can't concentrate on
either one. He just keeps swapping ends, fighting the
hounds first and then the hair-puller. That way, you
keep most of your hounds from getting killed, and the
hunter arrives with the rifle to get his bear."

Dad took his eyes off the road and looked at his
son with some surprise. "Maybe doing all that reading
does you some good at that, D.J. Say! I got me an
idee! Long's we're on the road, let's drive into town

and show the Widow Higgins our dogs!"

"Ah, Dad! Don't go there!"

"We're a'going, D.J.! And you be nice to that there little Priscilla of hers or I'll whang you good when we get home. You hear?"

D.J. nodded miserably and slumped in the seat. Grandpa Dillon had said the widow had set her cap for Dad, but Dad said he wasn't going to marry Hannah Higgins. Dad had worked with her husband in the woods before he got killed in a logging accident. Mrs. Higgins was a good housekeeper who set a fine table. Dad always managed to show up about suppertime. Mountain hospitality required feeding visitors, D.J. knew. But he'd have problems with the 9-year-old daughter. As always, she'd find a way to get D.J. in some kind of hot water. He had a right to feel miserable.

Dad parked the pickup on the quiet side street and cut the wheels sharply to the curb so the truck wouldn't roll down the steep hill. D.J. followed his father up the concrete steps to the neat white frame house with the green shutters. Dad knocked and the front door opened. Through the screen, Mrs. Higgins' blue eyes opened wide and she jerked her hand nervously to run it across her short blond hair.

Right away, D.J. knew something was wrong. He didn't know what it was, but it didn't take long to find out.

Chapter Three

A DEFENDER FOR THE OUTLAW BEAR

Mrs. Higgins said, "Why, Sam Dillon! And D.J.!
What a surprise to see you!" She didn't open the
screen door, which was most unusual. But Dad
didn't seem to notice.

"Hannah, we've been hit by an outlaw bear, so we
traded for some hounds."

"Mercy! A *bear!*" The way Mrs. Higgins said it,
the bear might have been coming down the street. D.J.
wondered why she was so nervous. He saw her turn
her head slightly and look behind her.

Nine-year-old Priscilla Higgins came up behind
her mother and looked through the screen door at D.J.
She made a face at him. Her hair was brown like her
eyes, but the hair looked like an eagle's nest that had
fallen on a fence post. It was the only untidy thing
about her.

D.J. made sure his dad and Mrs. Higgins weren't
looking, then made a face back at Pris. But Dad looked

down and caught D.J., as always. Dad dropped a powerful hand on the boy's shoulder and gave him a warning look. D.J. caught the fragrance of fried chicken and apple cobbler. Mrs. Higgins was getting supper, but she didn't invite her unexpected visitors inside.

D.J. heard heavy footsteps inside the living room. A giant of a man appeared beside Mrs. Higgins. D.J. caught the rumble of a mighty voice in a big chest as the stranger spoke.

"Did I hear somebody mention bears?"

D.J. saw Mrs. Higgins' hands flutter nervously. She stammered, "Oh, uh . . . yes. Uh . . . Sam, this here's . . . well, . . . he's a friend of ol' Miz Talbott's from church. She asked him to stop by. Paul, this is Sam Dillon and his boy, D.J."

The giant pushed the screen door open and extended a right hand the size of a picnic ham. "Howdy, Sam! I'm Paul Stagg. New to town. Mighty proud to know you."

Sam Dillon ignored the outstretched hand. His forehead wrinkled and he glanced quickly at the widow. She was very upset, twisting her flowered yellow apron with both hands. D.J. figured his dad was upset at finding a stranger there.

The giant didn't seem to notice Dad ignoring his hand. The stranger bent and shook D.J.'s hand. "D.J., is it?"

"It's really David . . . David Jonathan, but my friends call me D.J."

"Both mighty good Bible names! Especially David. You know David in the Bible fought bears and lions when he wasn't much more than your age. Sam, did

you know that when you and your missus named
your son?"

D.J.'s eyes followed the giant as he stood upright
again and faced Dad. The boy was reminded of a little
banty rooster facing a 16-hands* high stallion. Paul
Stagg was about 6'4", D.J. figured. He wore polished
saddle-colored cowboy boots and held a white 10-
gallon Stetson. With boots and hat, D.J. figured the
man was 7 feet tall. His hair was reddish. He wore
an old but clean cowboy shirt and blue jeans. D.J. figured the giant was about the nicest-looking man
he'd ever seen.

D.J. had made a mistake in taking his eyes off Pris.
She had slipped out of the house and kicked him
sharply on his right shin as everyone looked at the
two men.

"Ouch!" D.J. exclaimed.

Everyone looked at him. Pris was looking innocent as an angel in church. Her brown eyes were
watching a bee working on a red flower growing
against the porch rail.

"Bumped my leg," D.J. lied, rubbing the spot.

The giant said heartily, "Sam, did I hear you say
something about a bear?"

Sam Dillon was still suspicious. "You ever hunt
them?"

"All my life until recently."

Dad's anger vanished. His face broke into a smile.
He reached out his right hand. "Well, now, howdy,
Paul! I sure admire meeting up with another bear
hunter!"

The big man grinned and stuck out his right
hand. But before their hands touched, Pris piped up.

"Brother Paul's the new preacher!"

Dad snatched his hand back as fast as if he'd been snakebit. "Preacher?" Dad exploded.

"Lay preacher," the giant rumbled. He kept his big hand sticking out toward Dad. Paul Stagg didn't seem to notice Dad's tone. "I got a call to come re-open the community church here. But in my hunting days, I took 40 bears myself and was in on hunts where another 40 or so was taken."

D.J. was surprised at how his dad's manner changed. He reached out his right hand and gripped Paul Stagg's heartily. D.J. knew Dad was probably squeezing hard. He was such a short man that any-body who stood head and shoulders above him always made Dad try to show off his great strength.

"Where'd you hunt, Paul?" Dad asked, pumping the preacher's hand.

D.J. saw the widow sigh and smile. She invited the Dillons in and indicated seats. Dad headed for his fa-vorite wingback chair which had been Pris' father's, but the giant beat Dad to it. The preacher didn't seem to notice as he called toward the kitchen.

"Kathy, can you come out here a minute? I want you to meet some friends of Mrs. Higgins and her daughter."

D.J. had started to sit down on a footstool when a girl about 12 entered the room. She was very slender and already tall for her age. She dried her hands on a red apron as Paul Stagg said, "Gentlemen, this here's my daughter Kathy. Been helping in the kitchen."

D.J. briefly met the girl's blue eyes. Her hair was reddish like her father's and she had zillions of freck-les. D.J. said, "Hi," and she answered the same way.

She gave him and Dad the biggest smile D.J. had ever seen. "Excuse me," she said, "I'm helping with supper." She returned to the kitchen.

Dad asked, "Mrs. Stagg in the kitchen too?"

The preacher said, "No. Her father took sick and she went to help out awhile. She'll be back with us pretty soon, I reckon. Kathy'll go to school here this fall while I pastor for a while. Your missus with you, Sam?"

"My wife died last winter."

The giant reached out and gently touched Dad on the arm. "I'm right sorry, Sam."

Mrs. Higgins broke in. "Brother Paul is visiting all the people, inviting them to Sunday services. That's why he came here." She spoke directly to Sam Dillon. "The church has been closed since the last supply pastor left months ago. Now we'll have regular services again."

The preacher's voice rumbled up from his deep throat. "You're all welcome anytime. Sure do hope you all will come next Sunday. Say, David, speaking of bears—you want to hear a bear story?"

"Sure would," D.J. replied, looking up and smiling. "But you can call me 'D.J.' "

Mrs. Higgins said, "D.J.'s going to be a writer when he grows up. Write books and things. Maybe he can use your story in a book someday, Brother Paul."

"Well, he's welcome to it if he wants."

D.J. leaned forward, suddenly very glad he'd met this man. He sure hoped his father would be nice to the preacher.

Paul Stagg crossed his legs, leaned back in the

chair and tossed his white cowboy hat over the shiny
brown boot toe. "The trouble with telling bear stories,"
he said, hooking his hands behind his head, "is that
I got to get warmed up. You that way too, Sam?"

Dad shrugged and answer, "I don't tell many stories anymore."

Paul grinned, a wide, friendly grin that seemed to
light up the whole room. "Now you know it's true a
preacher won't lie, but like fishermen, bear hunters
are known to stretch the truth plumb out of shape.
Why, once I was telling a bear story to a man I'd met
while two of my old hunting partners—Jake and
Fred—was listening. When I finished up, Jake said,
'Paul, I wisht I'd a'been on that hunt.' Fred punched
Jake in the ribs and said, 'Hush up! You *was!*'"

Everyone laughed. D.J. could see the big man was
warming up. Paul continued, "People are always asking me about the biggest bear I ever saw. Well, we
run this old bear all day, but lost him about sundown.
So we found an old vacant cabin and stayed all night
because it was pretty cold. Well, sir, along in the night
I heard this scratching on the winder. I got up, took
a flashlight, and shined it toward the sound.

"There was a bear looking in the winder with a
head so big it looked like a bushel basket. Well, it was
too cold and I was too tired to do anything about it,
so I crawled back into bed. I didn't think much about it
until I happened to remember I was sleeping
upstairs."

Everyone exploded into laughter. D.J. noticed that
even his dad joined in. He seemed to have forgotten
about Tinsley Abst and Nails.

Dad got into the mood and began telling stories.

Mrs. Higgins laughed with relief, patted D.J. on the head, and said supper would soon be ready. She went into the kitchen while the men continued to swap bear stories. D.J. listened to them talk about the outlaw bear. D.J. spoke up and told about the lump he'd seen on the outlaw's jaw.

Paul nodded. "Don't you know that old bear must be really hurting from a bad tooth or sore jaw? Maybe a gunshot wound."

Dad said, "Most likely the outlaw that hit us can't eat natural food anymore. Hunger's driven him down to people country where there's garbage and turkey mash and shoats, like ours. Pain makes a bear mean, and he might hurt somebody."

The men agreed bears usually didn't bother humans unless those people came upon a sow with cubs. Paul said the greatest danger was in hunting through rough terrain or with unfamiliar dogs. D.J. glanced at Dad to see if he'd say anything about that, but the giant said something about a famous old bear named Ephraim. This bear had roamed over California and Nevada and some even said as far as Utah. Somebody was supposed to have killed the bear in the high country and marked the spot as "Ephraim's Grave."

Dad admitted he'd heard the story but had never learned if it was true. D.J. asked why Paul had quit hunting bears.

The giant looked at the boy and smiled. "My daughter made me do that, more or less. She doesn't hold with killing things, especially bears. Says California's someday going to declare they're a valuable natural resource and not varmints, as they've always been. Kathy says bears will be protected by law and you'll not be able to keep a cub as I once did, or hunt without a license and then only in certain periods or seasons when it's legal to hunt."

Dad cussed softly, blaming the government for interfering in a man's private business. D.J. knew Dad cussed so often since Mom died that he hadn't even noticed what he'd said, and in front of a preacher too. D.J. wondered if Mom was right. Would God someday touch Dad and Grandpa both and change their hearts?

"Supper!" Mrs. Higgins came out of the kitchen and indicated where she wanted each person to sit.

When all six were seated, she said, "I've had a Christian upbringing, but Sam doesn't much care for such things. Brother Paul, I know where you stand. So—anybody as wants to return thanks, can. Anybody who don't want to don't have to."

Dad nodded and reached for the mashed potatoes. D.J. watched the preacher, his daughter, Mrs. Higgins, and Pris bow their heads. But D.J. saw Mrs. Higgins kept her eyes open so she didn't miss a move of Dad's arm. She was ready when he passed her the potatoes.

D.J. and Pris looked at each other. In all the times the boy and his father had eaten supper there, nothing had ever been said about returning thanks. D.J. had a funny feeling that the bear hunter turned preacher was going to make a difference somehow.

Conversation died down while everyone ate. D.J. found himself wanting to know more about the bear hunter and his daughter. Once D.J. had caught Kathy's bright blue eyes on him, and he'd felt his face grow warm.

D.J. swallowed the last of his second piece of chicken. "Paul, were you always a preacher?"

"Not hardly, Son! I was borned in Oklahoma and grew up with a meanness to fight and such like. But my mother kept a'praying fer me, and one night I went down to the local brush arbor and got right with the Lord. Had a call to preach, but didn't have no reg'lar learning, so I've just been a'traveling around lay preaching where I can. Heard the local church here was closed, so I come and opened it with the help of fine people like Mrs. Higgins here."

D.J. got so interested he forgot Pris until he felt a hard kick on his shin. "Ouch!" he cried, looking at Pris. She was innocently looking the other way.

Dad demanded angrily, "D.J., what's the matter with you?"

D.J. lied again. "Bumped my knee on the table."

"Well," Dad said, "maybe you won't bump into anything twice if you're in the kitchen helping with dishes after supper."

Mrs. Higgins protested, but Dad was firm. "D.J.'ll be glad to do that and your little Pris can rest."

Paul said, "Kathy'll be glad to help, won't you, Honey?"

She nodded and got up from the table to clear it. D.J. stood and helped. The adults started talking. The boy saw Pris peeking out from under her eagle's nest of hair. She gave him a smug look. He wanted to get even with her, but there was no way. What a little pest she was! But Dad had always said she just wanted attention and D.J. should ignore her.

Kathy washed and D.J. dried. Kathy tossed her

long reddish-colored hair so her face was free and she could see D.J. better. She said, "You're going to be a writer when you grow up?"

"Guess so." He wiped a plate and set it on the lower shelf of the cupboard. "What about you?"

"I'm going to help sick people."

"Like a nurse?"

"Maybe. Or maybe I'll help sick animals, like a vet. Maybe I could even help that bear with the sore jaw if I was already a vet."

D.J. scoffed. "People don't help bears! They shoot them!"

The girl spun so suddenly D.J. almost dropped the plate. "You'd shoot that old bear just because he's sick or old or something?"

D.J. saw the color rise in her cheeks. He felt his own grow warm under her angry gaze. "What's wrong with that?" he demanded.

"Everything! What if that was your father? Would you shoot him? No! So why not do the same for a bear? If a bear's old or sick or whatever, it could be trapped safely. Have a vet treat it. When the bear's all well again, take it to a new place and turn it loose! That's what I'd do!"

D.J. was surprised at her spunk. But he wasn't going to let any girl make him feel wrong. He said, "In the Bible, David the shepherd boy killed lions and bears. If the Bible says it's OK, then who're you to say different?"

She dropped the dishcloth in the pan and placed both hands on her hips. Her bright blue eyes snapped like her voice. "In those days, they didn't have any way of trapping and treating animals. But today we have!"

D.J. tried not to lower his eyes. "I read about a man in history named Grizzly Adams. He used to trap grizzlies up along the Tuolumne and the Stanislaus Rivers not far from here. Kept some for pets. But that was maybe a hundred years ago. Now we got only black bears, and—"

She interrupted, her voice firm. "If I were a boy, or a man, I'd catch that bear safely and let him go when he got well."

D.J. frowned. "Lots of men are hunting that ol' outlaw. Some will use guns and some dogs. In fact, today we met a professional bear hunter who's come to town because the reward's now so high. That bear will die, Kathy."

She turned to face him, her eyes bright with controlled emotion. "Not if someone helps him!"

"One boy couldn't do anything like that."

"He could if some man'd help him. Somebody like my father."

D.J. faced Kathy. "He won't hunt bears anymore; you made him quit."

"He would if it was for a good cause and not for killing."

D.J. lowered his eyes. He liked her spunk, but he didn't like the feeling that she was winning the argument. He said, "Hey! I think I hear the dogs acting up."

He released the four hounds from the back of the pickup and took them for a walk in a vacant field. When he put them back in the pickup, he reached for the hair-puller. It slurped a big, wet tongue across D.J.'s cheek.

"Hey! You cut that out, Dog! I don't want you and I don't like you! Now come on and take a walk!"

The ugly little mutt bounced around like a puppy, which he really almost still was. Ten months old, Boot had said. The hair-puller jumped into D.J.'s arms.

"Hey! Cut that out!" he said. He lowered the dog to the ground. The hair-puller raced away in a big circle. He tucked himself so low his stubby tail almost seemed to be dragging the ground.

Somebody laughed. D.J. turned around. Pris was pointing at the mutt. "Look at that, D.J.! He's going to scrub his tail right off! He's cute."

She stopped suddenly, her eyes settling on D.J.'s face. She cocked her head sideways. "Funny," she said.

"What is?" he demanded, scowling at her.

She shrugged. "Oh, nothing. I was just thinking what it would be like if you were my brother."

"I'm *not* your brother and I never will be!"

"Don't be so sure, Mr. Smarty! I heard Mom talking with some ladies at church one day. They asked if she was going to marry your dad someday, and she said she was thinking on it."

D.J. felt his stomach jump. "My dad won't *never* marry again! Mom's the only wife he ever had, and just because she's dead don't mean he's going to ever remarry!"

"I don't want my mother to marry your father, either, so there! But—well, once I heard Mom tell your father you should have a collie, like you want. And if *she* was your new mother, I bet she'd make your dad let you have that collie."

D.J. had been so mad he was looking around for a dirt clod to chunk at Pris, but he suddenly stopped. He looked at her real hard. "Your mom said that?"

"Yep! And you know what Kathy said just now?"

D.J. managed to swallow and say casually, "I don't care what she said."

"Then I won't tell you." Pris started for the house.

D.J. ran after her, the hair-puller jumping up and whining beside him. "What'd she say?"

Pris stopped, cocked her head, and looked at him like a dog. "She said she thinks you're kinda cute."

D.J. let out a squall like he'd burned himself on a hot stove. He bent over and picked up a pine cone. Pris ran screeching toward the house. The boy threw the pine cone, but it fell far short. The mutt ran over and tried to pick it up, but the sharp points made him drop it.

"Dumb dog!" D.J. muttered. Yet he felt better than he had for days as he walked back toward the house. But he should have known the good feeling couldn't last.

Chapter Four

SURPRISE ON THE FIRST BEAR HUNT

It was dark when Sam Dillon eased the pickup across the shallow creek and up the hill to the Dillons' house. D.J. saw his grandfather in the truck's lights. He was sitting in his rocker on the front porch. The hounds bayed Grandpa from the back of the pickup.

D.J. whispered, "He's mad, Dad. Look at the way he's rocking!"

The old man rocked so hard the chair suddenly crashed over backward. Grandpa rolled over quickly, muttering in anger. He used his shillelagh to try regaining his feet. But when he couldn't rise, Grandpa whacked the upside-down rocker with the black-thorn cane.

D.J. laughed when he knew Grandpa wasn't hurt. The old man got to his feet and called out. "Been eating over at that there widder woman's again, I'll bet! Leaving a body here all alone to starve or eat his own cooking! Hey! What's them?"

Dad said, "Hounds! Trail hounds to catch that outlaw bear and give us the bounty money!"

Grandpa pulled himself up against the front porch post and looked at the hounds by the pale light of the front porch bulb.

Dad tied the hounds to the supports under the porch. He asked, "You a'fixing to find fault with my dogs?"

Grandpa clicked his false teeth and adjusted his bifocals. "No, Sam. I was just a'studying what to name them."

Dad yelled, "They already got names!" He pointed to the hound he was just chaining up. "That there black and tan is named Rock. He's got a beautiful voice on the trail."

D.J. smiled. Dad was repeating Boot Malloy because Dad hadn't even heard that hound whine yet.

Grandpa didn't say anything. Dad pointed. "That there mixed redbone and blue tick, well, that's Thunder. That one's Max, and the female is Roxie."

Grandpa didn't seem to hear him. He leaned over the porch rail and pointed with his cane. "That there first one'll be Blackie. The second one's Sally. . . ."

"Sally?" Dad yelled. The dogs scooted back under the porch. "Thunder's no female dog, and Sally's a female name!"

Grandpa didn't hear any better than a post when he took a mind to be contrary. "The third one is Jonesy, and the female's called Birdie!"

Dad looked like a balloon filling with water and about to burst. Grandpa didn't seem to notice. He sat down in his rocker. He had spoken. The hounds were named, and nothing Dad could say would change the old man's mind.

D.J. said, "Grandpa, what's this one?" The boy waved his hand toward the hair-puller which had been chained to the side of the porch nearer the back door.

Grandpa hobbled to the edge of the porch. "Hm! Don't rightly 'pear to me to be much. I'd say he's a nought, a cipher, a nothing dog."

D.J. didn't care for the mutt, but he didn't like those names. "Ah, Grandpa, he's not real handsome, I'll admit, but he should have a better name, don't you think?"

"Nope, D.J., I don't. He's a zero in my book. Likely no good for anything. I can see it in him right off. So that's his name: Zero."

Grandpa had spoken. D.J. didn't like the name, but there was nothing he could do about it unless Grandpa changed his mind. The boy looked at the mixed hound, Airedale, and Australian shepherd and sighed. Then he remembered what Boot Malloy had tried to tell Dad about why he shouldn't trade for that mutt, and D.J. had a funny feeling Grandpa might be right.

* * * * *

When the boy got home from fishing alone the next afternoon, he carried in an armload of white oak wood for the stove. He was surprised to see his father already home from work.

Dad said, "Get dressed, D.J.! We're going after that there outlaw bear!"

Grandpa exclaimed, "Sam, you can't possibly catch up to Ol' Satchel Foot tonight! That means you'll be out tomorrow too, and you'll get fired if you miss work!"

"We'll be back in time." Dad tamped kitchen
matches into an empty shotgun shell and poured melted paraffin over the top. D.J. knew that when it
cooled, the matches would be waterproofed. The paraffin could also be used to help start a fire if they ran
out of little stub candles carried for that purpose.

D.J. pulled on his "tin pants" like all the loggers
wore. These were of heavy canvas or brown ducking
that came up to his waist. Tin pants were never
washed. They had gotten so greasy they would stand
up by themselves. A person could run through the
brush with such tough clothing.

Grandpa snorted. "Sam, you're letting this bear
get to you."

"It's not just that he killed our shoat! It's the prin-
ciple of the thing."

"And the reward," Grandpa said.

D.J. laced up his high-top logging boots that came
up above his calves. He stood up on the hobnailed
boots with leather soles. They'd grip almost anything
from a log to a bare rock. He walked carefully so the
floor wouldn't be pitted by the hobnails.

Dad was checking his Springfield Ought Six.*
Like the Ought Three D.J. would carry, both had been
.30 caliber military rifles used before World War I.
Dad liked the long-barrelled Krag he'd fired at the bear
when it raided them, but it was too awkward in the
brush.

Dad admitted, "The reward's nice, but we also got
to get a move on. Met a professional bear hunter who's
come in with his kid to take that bear. Name of Abst.
Mean as a rattlesnake at shedding time. Got to beat

him to that bounty." Dad checked half a dozen shells he always hand loaded. They were called "roll your owns."

Grandpa laughed. "That there's the truth, Sam! You just can't abide having him beat you to that bear's hide."

"Doesn't matter what it is," Dad snapped. "Now leave me alone so I can think."

D.J. pulled on a red and white checkered flannel lumberjack shirt over his undershirt. Then he put on his tin coat. He tucked an old pair of brown jersey cotton gloves into one of the tin coat's deep pockets. Ordinarily, they were for cold weather, but they were also handy for moving brush. Dad didn't carry a canteen. Dad had said bear hunters depended upon finding water. There were so few people in the high country that any running stream was considered safe for drinking.

Prunes, raisins, and other dried fruits were stuffed into other deep pockets of the big tin coat. This was followed by jerky, salami, and other dried meats. Lastly, the boy added two chocolate bars. He did not carry a blanket. The idea was to go light. At night, Dad had said, bear hunters slept in their clothes. If it got really cold, hounds were piled on top of the hunters to get more warmth. But this was June, and all they'd need was a fire to lie down beside.

The boy picked up the heavy rifle. His mother had never approved of guns, but Dad had insisted D.J. learn to handle a weapon when he was old enough to learn safety. His father was a stickler for safety, and the boy was glad. D.J. had never killed anything, but he was a crack shot. He grabbed eight "roll your own" shells. He slipped an old soft felt brimmed hat on his head and looked at his father.

Grandpa shook his shillelagh at his son. "You're a'going off and leave me all alone out here!"

"The boogie man's not going to carry you off!"

D.J. wanted to yell, "Stop it! Stop it, both of you!" But he'd tried it before and it never did any good. Nothing seemed to work since Mom had died. Instead, he said, "I'm ready, Dad."

His father glanced up from where he was finishing tying his boots. "Get the dogs in the pickup."

"The hair-puller too?"

"Take 'em all. Let's find out what they're made of."

Grandpa sighed and sat down on the couch, his blackthorn stick clattering to the floor beside him. D.J. went to him and patted him on the shoulder. "You'll be OK, Grandpa."

The old man looked up and tried to smile. For the first time, D.J. sensed something was wrong. He bent over and asked softly, "You hurting, Grandpa?"

An old wrinkled hand covered with brown liver spots closed gently over D.J.'s hand. "Nothing but old age a'breathing down my neck."

The boy hesitated. "I don't have to go on that hunt, Grandpa."

"Not safe for a man to hunt alone. You go with your daddy. Look out after him."

D.J. frowned. "You sure?"

"I'm sure. Now go on."

D.J. patted his grandfather on the shoulder. He grunted and pulled back. D.J. saw the pain in the old man's face. "Grandpa, what's wrong?"

"Nothing. Now go on before your father hollers at you."

Dad drove D.J. and the dogs to a small turkey ranch where Dad had heard the outlaw bear had come the night before to eat the soft mash. They picked up the trail where the bear had ignored the turkeys but torn up several sacks of turkey feed. Rock, the "pappy" dog, sniffed along the cold bear trail and took off toward an apple orchard. Dad held two hounds on their chains while D.J. held the female hound and the little hair-puller.

Dad asked, "See how that old cold nose is working out that bear's scent? Going to jump Ol' Satchel Foot before sundown, with any luck."

D.J. was almost jogging to keep up with his father's untiring gait. The scruffy mutt was enjoying being with D.J. The dog ran at his side, rattling the chain and playfully nipping at D.J.'s ankles. The boy tried to shake him off and scold him, but the hair-puller seemed to think it was a game.

D.J. said, "Maybe Grandpa was right. You're a nothing dog and Zero's a good name for you."

It was nearing sundown when Dad paused to listen to the hound in the distance. "Trail's warming up, I think. I'll cut in this back-up hound. You be ready to unsnap that hair-puller when we hear these hounds are a'looking at that old bear."

The second hound was released and bounded away, baying with the joy of the chase. Dad was pleased. "Sounds to me like two mighty good hounds, D.J. Well, we'll soon know."

In a little while, Dad released the third hound and ordered D.J. to do the same with Roxie. The two hounds were anxious to join the two dogs baying on a hot trail ahead. Zero didn't seem at all interested, which made the boy a little curious.

D.J. looked at the sky, wondering how much longer they'd dare go on. Even with flashlights, it was dangerous to move in the blackness of the mountains.

"We'll stay within hearing distance," Dad said. "When the hounds bay that bear, we got to come to them. No sense turning them loose if you don't intend to come to them. Let's see how that little cut-across mongrel does."

Dusk was settling when they topped a pine-covered ridge and stopped again to listen to the hounds. Dad frowned. "Sounds like there's another dog's voice in there I don't recognize."

D.J. cocked his head and listened. He couldn't tell for sure, so he said nothing. But Dad was so sure that he started "cussing and caving," as Mom used to say.

Dad exclaimed, "Must be that Tinsley Abst's dog! Come on, D.J.! Let's run a little bit."

They were making their way through heavy brush when D.J. smelled wood smoke. "Dad?"

"I smell it. Must be we're coming up on that Zeering feller who lives hereabouts."

D.J. looked around sharply. "You mean the mad hermit?"

"You got that wrong, D.J. He's called the Hermit of Mad River. Mighty big difference. There's his shack! We got to stop a minute. Won't be neighborly not to and he might not take kindly to us passing without speaking. Besides, the hounds are still running that bear."

Zeke Zeering came out on the split-log front porch of a home he'd probably built himself. He held an old coal oil lantern high until Dad and D.J. introduced themselves. Then the old man lowered the light and invited the visitors up to his rickety front porch. He was a man of medium height, well along in years, and probably hadn't taken a whole lot of baths lately. D.J. wrinkled his nose a little.

Mr. Zeering said, "I don't git many visitors hereabouts." He scratched the front of his threadbare striped railroad coveralls where a patched blue workshirt showed. "Bear hunting, are you?"

"Most of those hounds you hear are mine," Dad admitted. "Seems like maybe another dog is running that trail too."

"That's my Tug. He's a hair-puller. Well, was, anyway. He's old and toothless and almost blind, like me. But he still likes to run a trail now and again."

Dad looked at D.J. with relief. "That's your dog's voice?"

"Purely is." The hermit bent to look at the scruffy little dog D.J. still had on a chain. "Say, there, Sonny, that's a mighty fine-looking dog you got there!"

Before D.J. could answer, Dad said, "That's a stock-killing bear they're running. Killed one of our pigs."

"You don't say? Well, I ain't got many comforts, but I'd be obliged if you and your boy come in and took supper with me."

"Thank you kindly, Mr. Zeering, but we got to keep up with our dogs. I want to be near enough to cut loose this hair-puller when he's needed."

The hermit nodded slowly. "I been living alone

back here near 20 years, I reckon. Don't miss people much. But sometimes—"

He paused and D.J. was aware the hermit's watery blue eyes had settled on him.

Dad prompted, "Sometimes what?"

"Sometimes I wisht I'da had me a son born. But I got nary chick nor kin. Well, thanks for stopping. And don't worry about Tug. He'll come in when he's ready."

They went on, using their flashlights. D.J. kept looking back. He wasn't sure what there was about that old hermit, but something bothered the boy. He felt sorry for Mr. Zeering. Old. Alone. Like that outlaw bear.

The thought surprised D.J. But before he could think about it any more, the evening air was filled with the sound of hounds baying excitedly.

"They're a'looking at him, D.J.! Unsnap that hair-puller!"

D.J. bent to obey. The little mutt jumped up to lick D.J.'s face. The boy pushed him away. But when the hair-puller was freed, he didn't bound off with joyful barks to join the bear chase as the hounds had.

D.J. pointed into the night. "Go!" he commanded. "Can't you hear those hounds? They're fighting Ol' Satchel Foot, and they need you!"

Zero wagged his stub tail and nearly twisted himself in two trying to please D.J. But even when Dad shouted at the mutt, the dog didn't run toward the hounds. Instead, he ran around D.J. in a joyful circle, nearly sitting on his tail in the brown pine needles that covered the ground.

Dad swore. "That there ain't no hair-puller! He

don't want to get in on that bear! He's no bear dog!
He's worthless! Wait'll I get my hands on that Boot
Malloy!"

"He tried to warn you, Dad."

"I don't care! D.J., your grandpa was right. That's
a nothing dog and he's well-named as Zero."

Father and son ran on, using their lights. Soon
they heard the hounds had 'treed' the bear. The closer
they got to the angry sounds of bear and dog's fighting, the closer Zero ran to the boy. Soon D.J. felt his
boots hitting the little mutt in the lower jaw with every step he took. The boy tried to make the dog move,
but Zero returned to running between the boy's legs
and almost underfoot. Dad was swearing so awful D.J.
was scared. All the words were aimed at that scruffy
little mongrel.

They came upon the bear and hound fight from
above. The lights showed Dad and D.J. were standing
on the top of a small cliff. Some 15 feet below, the
hounds were leaping and baying at a bear out of sight
under the cliff's lip. It was obvious the bear had
backed up against the cliff to protect his backside. The
five hounds, including the hermit's old hair-puller,
were churning up the dust and making an awful
racket.

Dad said, "I can't get a shot at him from here! I'll
have to work my way down. He'll kill my dogs unless I
get to them!" He glanced around. "You stay here,
D.J., and don't move! This here's decomposed granite
rock we're standing on. Don't jump around! I want
to know exactly where you are when I shoot."

In a little while, D.J.'s excitement got so great he
lay down on his stomach and crawled forward. He

peered over the top of the cliff, but couldn't see anything. He thought about using his flashlight, but it
might interfere with Dad's light when he was ready
to fire.

The little mutt ran up to the boy and licked his
face. D.J. rolled over and pushed the dog away. "You
cut that out! You hear? You're supposed to be down
there helping fight that bear!"

D.J. turned back and wiggled closer to the edge of
the cliff. He heard the hounds baying and jumping in
and out at the bear. His tusks clicked. Suddenly,
Zero ran and jumped right on the boy's back.

"You stop that!" D.J. rolled over hard and sat up
to shove the little mongrel away. But the boy stopped
his hands in midair. He felt the decomposed granite
cliff begin to crumble. Frantically, D.J. tried to jump to
safety. But Zero leaped into his arms.

Boy and dog fell straight down toward the middle
of that bear-and-hound fight!

Chapter Five

HOW TO RIDE A BEAR

D.J. didn't even have time to yell. In the darkness, he felt his feet touch something. His legs were forced apart. He landed hard like a rider leaping onto a galloping horse. Automatically, the boy let go of the dog and grabbed for something to hang onto. As his fingers closed about coarse, thick hair, D.J. shouted in surprise. He had landed on the bear's back!

The next instant, the boy was riding that bear backward as it streaked for the brush. All the hounds bayed after it. D.J.'s mind screamed, "Get off here any way you can!" But D.J.'s hands wouldn't let go of the bear's hide. He felt the hounds jumping and snapping at the bear, but they couldn't turn him. He was streaking for the brush. Above the barking and huffing and turmoil, D.J. heard the unmistakable sound of a rifle bolt working a shell into the firing chamber.

He started to yell, "Dad! Don't shoot!" but the bear

swung his head around and D.J. felt hot breath on his backside. He threw himself sideways, falling off the bear onto the brush and rocks. A yelping hound stepped on the boy's chest as he rolled, but the sounds told him the chase was going away from him.

D.J. scrambled on hands and knees to the shelter of a large boulder as a flashlight flickered. In the light beam, D.J. saw enough of the bear to know it wasn't the outlaw. This one was a small 200-pound cinnamon colored boar, or male. The boy also glimpsed the little hair-puller with his short tail tucked between his legs. The mutt was running flat-out scared away from the hounds and the bear, toward that flashlight. The light beam flickered down on the dog just a second before D.J. saw Zero run smack-dab into the front of Dad's legs.

Dad's angry yell came as he fell forward. The rifle exploded. The muzzle flash lit up the night. The hounds chased the bear into the darkness. A moment later, from the way they were baying, D.J. knew they'd forced the bear to climb a tree.

D.J. scrambled to his feet and ran toward the flashlight which had rolled part-way down a little hill. "Dad! Dad? You all right?"

"I . . . I hurt myself, I think. Get that flashlight and let's see. Don't pay no never-mind to that bear. The dogs'll keep him up that tree."

D.J. held the light while his father pulled up his tin pants to check his leg. The boy asked, "What happened?"

"That fool hair-puller made me fall and the rifle went off accidentally. And did you see why? That dog is afraid of bears! Now I know why Boot Malloy told me I didn't want that mutt!"

D.J. felt something touch his leg. He flipped the flashlight down. "Bad dog!" he cried at the sight of Zero. "You ran away and got Dad hurt!"

The mutt lowered his head and tucked his stub tail. Zero dropped to the ground and raised his big brown eyes to the boy. D.J. felt sorry for the little mutt.

Dad said, "Hold that light steady so's I can see. There." In a moment he spoke again. "I think maybe my right knee's knocked catty-wampus. Better camp here because I won't be able to walk out on this leg tonight."

"But the bear—"

Dad interrupted. "That's a young bear the hounds put up that tree. He won't come down so he's no danger to us. Better call off those hounds and chain them. Get a fire started."

When the flames were leaping high and the hounds were quiet, D.J. explained about the lip of the cliff caving in and him falling right on top of the bear.

Dad chuckled. "If you're going to ride bears, you'd best wear spurs! But as for that there ugly little hair-puller, well—he's *afraid* of bears! He's totally worthless. We got to get rid of him. Maybe I can unload him on that Abst feller."

"The Absts were at Boot Malloy's before we were, Dad. Maybe Mr. Abst knows the truth about Zero."

"Maybe. But we got to get rid of that dog."

D.J. was surprised to hear himself say, "Ah, Dad, maybe we should give him another chance."

"No! That mutt's no earthly good. He made you

fall off that cliff where the bear could've hurt you bad. That dog knocked me down and give me this here knee. I'll likely be off work a spell. That means Abst can chase that bear and take the reward all to himself. I've got half a notion to just leave that dumb beast here in these mountains!"

"Ah, Dad—"

"I won't have no cowardly bear-dog on the place! Now, build up that fire and let's get some sleep."

D.J. awoke in the night to find Zero had snuggled up against his head. The boy reached up to shove the scruffy little dog away. Instead, he gave Zero a little pat. "Well, just for tonight," D.J. whispered.

* * * * *

A few days later, Dad was sitting with his leg stretched out straight on the homemade bench. He was in a bad mood from missing work. Grandpa was sitting on the front porch in his rocker. D.J. was stretched out on the sofa trying to write a short story about a boy who rode a bear. He looked up at Grandpa and was surprised to see he was reading a small New Testament.

Suddenly, Zero barked sharply. For such a small dog, he had the loudest voice D.J.'d ever heard. Dad hadn't figured out how to get rid of the mutt. The hounds began baying and rattling their chains as they ran out from under the house.

D.J. sat up. "Somebody's coming!"

"See who it is, D.J."

The boy went to the front screen and looked out. Grandpa was rocking gently, looking toward the creek. There was no sign of the Bible, but D.J. saw a small square lump in the bib of his grandfather's overalls.

D.J. said, "It's Mrs. Higgins and Priscilla."

Grandpa whacked his Irish shillelagh angrily against the front porch floor. "I knew it! That there widder woman is a'coming to devil me! She'll want to fix up and clean and cook and make me look like a plumb fool!"

Dad shushed Grandpa and told D.J. to make the dogs be quiet. The boy called sharply through the open windows until the hounds quieted. Then he opened the front screen door and invited the visitors in. They spoke to Grandpa who just grunted and rocked hard. D.J. hoped the old man wouldn't go over backward again.

The visitors were seated on the sofa. D.J. took a seat on the other bench opposite Dad at the table. Mrs. Higgins indicated a big wicker basket she'd placed on the floor beside her. "This is extra food we had left over from the church supper last night. It's more than Pris or I can eat, so we thought maybe you folks might enjoy it."

Dad said, "You didn't need to come away out here to do that!"

Grandpa called from the front porch. "I should say not! Why, I'm as good a cook as any a'person here-abouts! You don't see my son nor grandson looking poorly, do you?"

The widow's face turned red. Her hands fluttered nervously. She protested, "Oh, my no, Mr. Dillon, sir! I didn't mean anything like that."

Dad interrupted. "Don't pay him no never-mind! He's just been having the miseries lately. D.J., why don't you take little Pris here and show her our new pups?"

D.J.'s eyes widened in alarm. Just then Pris made a face at him.

"Hound pups?" she asked.

D.J. sighed with relief. "Born yesterday. Not worth seeing much yet."

Mrs. Higgins said, "We can't stay anyway. We have to get back. Choir practice tonight."

Dad frowned. "You going to church in the middle of the week, Hannah?"

She seemed concerned that Dad understand. "I know how you feel about church and preachers and such, Sam, but Brother Paul's a mighty good man. Why, the church is packed out every Sunday morning, now. Isn't that right, Priscilla?"

"Sure is!" The girl looked at D.J. and said, "Everybody comes from school, practically. 'Cept you."

D.J. started to say he didn't go to church anymore, but his dad said it for him. "Besides," Dad continued, "there's no way for the boy to get there since ol' Miz Lummers got killed with my wife. Rest their souls."

"Sam, Pris and I came to bring that extra food, as I said, but we also want to invite all three of you to next Sunday's services. We'll drive by for you."

Grandpa bent over with laughter and pounded his cane on the floor. "That's a good one! Us go to church! Why, the whole earth'd probably fall apart if we did that!"

D.J. was surprised to hear Dad speak firmly to his father. "That'll be enough of that! Now," he said, turning back to Mrs. Higgins, "I don't care none about going, but if you're a mind to, D.J. here'll be ready and waiting at the bottom of the hill across the creek come Sunday go-to-meeting time."

* * * * *

That Sunday, D.J. found himself sitting in church next to some boys he knew from school. They whispered and passed notes, but D.J. was quiet. His eyes kept going to Kathy Stagg. Her reddish hair caught the sun through the open window. Once he saw her looking at him, but she lowered her eyes and looked away. D.J. wondered if she knew Priscilla had told him on the drive into town that Kathy was telling everybody he was the cutest boy in Stoney Ridge.

Paul Stagg was a powerful speaker. D.J. noticed that everyone had called him "Brother Paul." His giant's voice rumbled deep in his chest and came out to shake the little church's rafters. He was preaching on love.

"When Jesus was asked what was the greatest commandment, He said, 'Hear, O Stoney Ridge, you shall love the Lord your God with all your heart, and with all your soul, and with all your strength, and with all your mind' " (Luke 10:27).

The giant grinned. "Maybe Jesus didn't say 'Stoney Ridge' in your Bible, but that's what He meant for us today, right here in this place. Now open your Bibles. . . ."

D.J.'s mind wandered off. He wished he had a Bible. He'd never really cared before, but there was something about the way the big man said things that made D.J. curious.

Brother Paul had worked himself up into a pretty good voice when D.J.'s mind came back to hear what was being said. "Now we come to what they call 'application,' in preaching. That means, 'So what?

What does that mean to me?' Well, I'll tell you."

"More hungry, hurting strangers have been driven
from God's house by unsociable church people than by
the poorest preaching in the world! Because I love
you all, I can't stand by and let you do that—maybe
something you won't know till Judgment Day! So I'll
tell you flat-out what to do. Don't stand around in this
church and talk to your friends until you've found a
stranger. Greet him or her like you would your own
flesh and blood. But remember, the Bible tells us an-
gels sometimes come as strangers. So, after you've
howdied and shook, take him or her by the arm and
bring them to somebody else. Introduce them like your
kinfolks. Now, I'm a'going to say a prayer so you can
all go home to supper, but don't you dare go until you
see if you can find an angel disguised as a stranger."

The big man's good spirits and wide grin made
everyone act friendly. They fairly ran around the little
church, shaking hands and slapping each other on
the back and hugging. By the time D.J. got to the side
door, he felt as if his arm had been about shaken off.
Besides that, some of the women had tried to kiss him
on the cheek. He'd dodged them. A few of the men
had ruffled his hair which Dad had made him comb
carefully. D.J. slipped out the side door while everyone else filed by the big preacher to shake his hand.

The boy stood under a lightning-struck ponderosa
pine and looked at the church. It looked the same as
when he'd come there with his mother. The white
frame structure had been newly repainted. The June
sun glistened on a fresh coat of paint. The corrugat-
ed sheet iron roof was still rusted where the snows had
melted and run down for years. The open belfry was

pocked with thousands of holes where woodpeckers had stored acorns. The bell rope was new, however, and hung from the bell that could be heard for miles.

But something was different too, D.J. knew. Maybe it was the singing. His mother had always sung in church. Sometimes she'd played the guitar. Whatever it was, the boy felt a warm niceness he couldn't explain.

Suddenly, he heard loud laughter. He turned to see Nails Abst standing by his father's black pickup truck at the curb. "I knew it!" the older boy yelled. "You go to church and sit with the women!"

D.J. swallowed hard. "I go where I want, and nobody stops me!"

Nails worked his rough-looking hands. "I know somebody who can make you wish you'd stayed inside with the women and little kids!"

D.J. started to answer when he sensed someone come up behind him. He turned his head to see the lay preacher's daughter standing beside him.

Kathy Stagg said softly, "Don't pay any attention to that bully. Mom and Dad sent me with a message for you. They say you're invited to take supper with us today."

"I can't. I got to ride home with Mrs. Higgins."

"Daddy says he'll see you get home before nightfall."

"Well, I'd like to, but my dad and grandpa would worry."

"No, they won't. Dad had Mrs. Higgins tell your folks you'd probably stay for supper with us."

"You sure?"

"I'm sure." She lowered her eyes and the reddish hair fell across her face, hiding it from the boy.

He hesitated. "Well," he said finally, "I guess it's OK. Maybe he'll tell me some more bear stories."

As D.J. started toward the church with Kathy, he heard Nails Abst's rough laughter and some jeering words. *Someday,* D.J. thought, *I'm going to have to deal with that guy, even if he is stronger than I am.*

D.J. MAKES A DANGEROUS DECISION

Kathy's mother twisted in the front seat of her husband's aging green sedan. Her blue-green eyes sparkled and her smile was warm. "I'm so glad you could join us, D.J.!" she said. She was a pretty woman, quite slender, with short brunette hair and a dimple in her right cheek.

"Thanks for inviting me," D.J. said. He stole a glance at Kathy sitting beside him. She was looking out the window at some beehives in an apple orchard they were passing.

Mrs. Stagg asked, "Paul told me about your father and grandfather. I trust they're well?"

"Yes, thanks, except Dad's leg isn't healing too fast. He's been off work several days. With no money coming in, he gets to fretting some." D.J. paused, then remembered to ask, "How's your father?"

"Better. My mother wrote this week that he is recovering nicely. It was good to be with my parents for a while, even if it did mean leaving Paul and Kathy alone." She paused, then continued. "I understand you used to go to church with your mother?"

The boy didn't answer for a moment. Finally he said, "I went when we had a supply pastor. But I quit when Mom got hurt in the accident. I asked God to heal her, but she died." He looked out the window.

Mrs. Stagg said, "D.J., there are some things no human can rightly explain. But you shouldn't give up your faith in God because of that. Someday, maybe, you'll understand."

"Maybe," the boy admitted, still looking out the window, but not seeing anything. "But I don't know. I'm not even sure He really exists."

Paul Stagg's deep rumbling voice filled the car. "Lots of young people your age go through a period of doubting. I did. But when I look at the stars and these mountains and even at a snowflake, I know Someone made them and put everything in place. I can't look around me without believing—without knowing, really—that there is a God and He loves us all. So I believe, even though I can't always understand. D.J., I hope you come to that time too."

The boy was silent a moment. He remembered how his mother had taught him about Jesus. She had taught him to read the Bible and how to pray.

Kathy asked, "Do your father and grandfather ever go to church?"

D.J. turned to face Kathy. "Mom told me once that Dad used to go to church with her before they were married. But he got mad at something or somebody in the church and never went back. And I'm not sure about Grandpa. I think he used to believe, but he never talks about it."

Paul Stagg said, "Can't always tell what a person's thinking inside, D.J. We're all praying for your family and you."

D.J. squirmed a little. He didn't want to talk about such things. But his mind leaped back and he saw his mother as she had been.

She cooked and sewed and kept Dad and Grandpa from arguing. Sometimes she'd take up her guitar and play and sing, mostly hymns. And she laughed. When she laughed, Dad and Grandpa and D.J. laughed too. She had made their home happy, and she always told D.J. that no matter how bad things looked, God would always work them out if you believed and had patience. But she was dead and D.J. was lonely and he didn't see how any good could come out of that.

The Stagg home was a rental two miles outside of town. The house was small, but D.J. had an instant feeling the place was special. Flowers had already been planted. Dry weeds had been cut and carried away. Untended vines were trimmed back.

Inside, the house smelled clean and warm. It echoed with happy sounds. D.J. heard Kathy and her mother laughing in the kitchen as they prepared lunch. D.J. sat down on a comfortable green couch with cheery yellow flowers in the pattern. Paul Stagg sank into a tan-colored easy chair that looked like leather, but D.J. guessed really wasn't. The giant leaned back and asked, "You like to hear some more bear stories?"

"Sure! Got any funny ones?"

"Well, now, you got to remember what I said once

about stretching the truth some. I wouldn't want you to get the idea I'm not a truthful preacher."

"I'll remember." He returned the giant's grin.

"Let's see . . . oh, yes—it all started when a farmer came to me because he wanted me to get an ol' bear that was eating up his corn. It had just come to roasting ear size for eating. So I went over there to take a look at the bear tracks the farmer told me about. It was too late to do anything that day, so I went away to sleep and came back just before daylight.

"I barely got hid real good when I saw that old bear coming out of the woods. Well, sir, he hopped over a rail fence and started down the rows of corn. But this ol' bear stood up on his hind feet and laid those ears of corn in his arm just like a man gathering firewood to carry into the house. That got me curious, so I didn't shoot. I just watched.

"When that bear got a big armload of corn, he turned, still walking upright like a man, hopped over that fence and went off about a hundred yards. It was light enough now I could see somebody'd cut a big tree down and left a stump that rotted out. I watched as that bear tossed his armload of corn into that hollow stump.

"I wasn't sure if the bear was storing corn for the winter or what, so I waited. When the bear walked over the hill and out of sight, I went over to the stump and took a look. You know what I saw? That bear had two pigs in there he was fattening up!"

D.J. roared with laughter. "That's a good one!"

The giant grinned with delight. "You understand that I can't rightly testify to the whole truth of that there particular story. But I can tell you some stories that you may not believe."

The lay preacher continued to tell stories until Kathy came in to set the table and announce lunch was ready. D.J. was given a straight-backed wooden chair across from Kathy. Mrs. Stagg sat at the end of the table nearest the kitchen. Paul Stagg took the other end of the table. He reached out and engulfed D.J.'s right hand while Mrs. Stagg took the other. The boy saw that Kathy held her parents' hands so the circle was complete. The big man's voice rumbled a bass prayer of thanks. D.J. didn't close his eyes. He was thinking how nice it was to have a white linen table-cloth instead of printed oilcloth.

That was the happiest meal he'd had in months. Everyone laughed and talked, sometimes all at once. D.J. had second helpings of pot roast with boiled po-tatoes and two slices of German chocolate cake for des-sert. Finally, he picked up his cloth napkin, used it, and leaned back.

"That was the best cooking I've had in a long time," he said happily.

"Have some more," Paul Stagg urged.

"No, thanks. I've had plenty."

Mrs. Stagg asked, "You lived here all your life, D.J.?"

"Born in the hospital at Indian Springs. That's the county seat."

"You going to live here always?" Kathy asked.

"No. Soon's I can, I'm moving away."

"Where you going?" the girl asked.

"I don't know. I'm going to move right out of high school, and I'm never coming back!"

Kathy exclaimed, "Why not? Stoney Ridge is the

nicest place we ever lived! If Dad didn't have to go
preach wherever the Lord calls him, we'd stay right
here forever! Wouldn't we, Dad? Mom?"

Her parents nodded, but D.J. hardly noticed. He
said with feeling, "I hate this place! I hate where we
live! I hate my Dad and Grandpa fighting and I hate
not having a collie or a boy my own age for a friend!"

The three Stagg family members looked at him in
surprise. D.J. lowered his head, but his feelings didn't
change.

Paul Stagg said quietly, "David, we can't always
choose our circumstances or our surroundings. But
God doesn't make any mistakes. He puts us all in a
place for a reason."

D.J. shrugged and looked at his plate. He wished
the laughter and stories hadn't stopped.

Paul Stagg continued. "I used to be ashamed of
my heritage; of where I came from and my folks and
all. They were Oklahoma tenant farmers with only a
sixth-grade education. But the Lord made me see that
He'd had me born to my folks for a reason, and born
in the place where I was. Without that background, I'd
not be able to enjoy life the way I do today. Fact is,
D.J., I'm proud to be what I am: a plain ol' country boy
who loves and serves the Lord."

D.J. shifted uneasily in his chair. He didn't like all
this talk. Kathy seemed to sense this. She announced
unexpectedly, "I'm going to church camp next week.
You ever been to one?"

"No. Never been anywhere."

"Would you like to go?" she asked.

"Can't. I've been studying on it, and I've come up
with a decision. You see, it's my fault that Dad got hurt

and can't work. Doctor bills piling up too."

Paul exclaimed, "D.J., you can't be blamed for that!"

"If I'd not tried to get too close to the top of that cliff and look over, and if that dumb ol' dog hadn't jumped on my back and then run away, Dad wouldn't be hurt. Dad's trying to sell that mutt, or give him away. And I've got to go after that outlaw bear."

Kathy protested, "D.J., you can't do that!"

Her mother agreed. "It's impossible for one boy to take on that responsibility. Do your father and grandfather know about this?"

"No'm. Haven't told them yet. I figured on just taking the hounds one day and slipping out quiet-like and doing it."

The giant's rumbling voice was next. "D.J., you can't take that risk!"

"Got to," the boy insisted. "That's the only way I can make up for things."

Paul frowned thoughtfully. "Maybe you should give that heeler another chance. Dogs sometimes are like a boy; deserve a second chance."

"No chance for that mutt," D.J. said firmly. "Dad said we're getting rid of him, and that's the way it is. Mom used to say nobody was as contrary-minded as my dad when he set his mind on something. So we got to sell that mutt, and I've got to get to hunting that bear. I have to hurry too because that Mr. Abst and his boy are racing to beat me to killing that outlaw bear."

Paul sat up straight. "David, no offense, but you're not yet a full-grown boy, and bear hunting's dangerous for even two or three men!"

"No choice," he said quietly.

Mrs. Stagg looked across the table at her husband. "Paul, can't you get someone from the church to help D.J.?"

"No experienced bear hunters around; leastwise, none I'd feel good about trusting this boy's life to."

Kathy reached across and touched her father's big hand. "You could go with him, Dad."

D.J. glanced up in surprise. Kathy's parents were no less surprised. D.J. blurted, "I thought you were against killing bears!"

"I am." Kathy tilted her chin defiantly and looked steadily at him. "But Dad has a permit to trap a nuisance bear that's been raiding the church camp. He already has a man making a culvert trap for that bear. I've read the bounty posters, and it doesn't say anything about the outlaw bear having to be dead. The reward would be paid for the live bear as long as he was trucked so far away he'd never come back here. So why couldn't both that outlaw and the nuisance bear be trapped?"

D.J. started to say he thought that was the dumbest thing he'd ever heard. Why was it that Kathy had to be so spunky and always making him feel like he had to defend everything he believed?

Before the boy could decide what to say, the lay preacher answered his daughter's question. "I'd love to, Kathy, but I can't. Got the Lord's work to look after, plus catching that church-camp raider before all those kids arrive."

D.J. was relieved. He'd grown up in an area where wild game was shot for food or sport, and nuisance animals were always killed. That was the only thing he'd ever heard about. Nobody ever had made a suggestion like Kathy's. Boy! She made him about half-mad, always disagreeing with him.

On the way back into town with Paul Stagg, the big man said he thought he had a low tire. He stopped at the town's only gas station and checked the air pressure. D.J. went around back to the restroom.

Nails Abst was just coming out of the washroom. His scraggly hair fell wetly from his forehead and half-way down the bridge of his nose. "Well, now! Look who's here! D.J., the church boy!"

D.J. tried to push by without answering, but Nails moved sideways and blocked his path. "Hey! I just thought of something! My pop and me lost our hair-puller to that outlaw bear a couple a'nights ago. We'll take yours."

For a moment, D.J. was too surprised to speak. Though the Absts had been to Boot Malloy's place, they hadn't known the truth about the hair-pulling bear dog. Here was a chance to unload that coward on them.

D.J. said, "He's not for sale."

Nails sneered. "Dog's probably no-account any-way. But it don't matter none. Soon's my pop and me kill that outlaw bear, we'll have plenty of money to buy all kinds of hair-pullers."

D.J. watched Nails walk away. Suddenly, without having any idea why he said it, he called out. "You're not going to kill that bear!"

Nails turned. "Why not?"

"Because," D.J. exclaimed, "that bear's going to be captured alive and trucked out of here!"

"Who's going to do a dumb thing like that?"

"I am!" D.J.'s stubbornness was getting away from him. He hadn't meant to say that.

"*You?*" Nails pointed at the mountain boy.

D.J. wished he hadn't blurted out such a thing. The older boy laughed. "That's stupid! Plain stupid! Wait'll I tell my pop how dumb you really are."

D.J. could hear Nails laughing halfway down the street. D.J. groaned. He wet his hands in the sink and pumped the harsh soap granules onto his palms. He thought, *Boy! Now I've done it!*

Chapter Seven

A MAD MOTHER BEAR WITH CUBS

Just as the sun was setting in a saddle of the western range, Paul Stagg dropped D.J. at the bottom of the hill where the Dillons lived. D.J. slid out of the car onto the shoulder of the road. "Well, thanks again," he said.

"It pleasured us to have you with us. And don't worry about what you said to that young Abst fellow. Soon's I trap that nuisance bear at the church camp, you can borrow the trap and try for Ol' Satchel Foot. Just hope it won't be too late, D.J."

"Me too," the boy said. He waved good-bye, crossed the road, and sat down on a boulder to take off his shoes and socks. He waded the creek by the twin poplars and walked barefooted up the rutted trail. The hounds bayed him, but quieted when he spoke to them. They went back under the high front porch.

But not Zero. He was chained beyond the hounds, closer to the back door. The little mutt ran to the end of his chain and danced on his hind legs. His forepaws

75

moved in the air, trying to reach the boy. The scruffy mongrel dog seemed determined to twist himself in two with gladness. D.J. spoke firmly. "Quiet! Or I will sell you to the Absts."

Grandpa had been sitting quietly in his rocking chair until the dogs disturbed him. He raised his gray head. D.J. smiled and called, "Hi, Grandpa," but the old man didn't answer. The boy climbed the steps and looked into the faded blue eyes. "You OK, Grandpa?"

"Sure," the old man said quietly, without looking up. Grandpa started rocking, very slowly, the chair squeaking. The old man's eyes didn't meet his grandson's, but seemed to be looking off into the distance. It gave D.J. an uneasy feeling he couldn't explain. He hesitated, unsure of what to say or do next.

Dad's voice came from inside the living room. "He's feeling poorly again. Got the miseries just about everyplace a man can have. Now, where you been all day?"

"You know where I've been," D.J. said, entering the house.

Dad's voice snapped. "Don't sass me!"

D.J. said softly, "I wasn't sassing, Dad. You said I could take supper with the preacher—the bear hunter—after church. He just dropped me off."

Dad looked up from where he was rolling his own rifle cartridges. "I didn't expect you to be gone all day. Did you find someone to buy that dog?"

"No." D.J. said it before remembering what Nails Abst had said. But Nails hadn't said anything about buying the hair-puller.

Dad muttered, "I'm getting tired of feeding him!

But right now you feed the the hogs and hounds."

D.J. said, "Yes, sir," and swallowed hard. The good feeling he'd had with the happy Stagg family was swept away. The boy wanted to talk about trapping the outlaw bear. But Dad wasn't in a good mood. D.J. asked, "How's your leg?"

"You can see how it is!" Dad snapped. His leg was propped up stiffly on a pillow supported on the table bench. "Now you get out of your good clothes and do the chores."

D.J. thought of how nicely everyone spoke in Paul Stagg's house. D.J. wished his family talked politely instead of always biting and growling. It was hard to imagine his mother being right when she said someday Jesus would touch Dad's and Grandpa's hearts and they'd be changed. If God could do that, maybe D.J. would believe again.

He removed his good clothes in the bathroom and put on his patched overalls. Barefooted, he went through the living room into the kitchen and outside the back door. He reached into the pump house for the cracklings.* He carried the dog food back toward the dogs. Zero was closest. The mutt squeezed from under the low end of the porch and bounded to the end of his chain again.

D.J. pulled out the dog's old pie plate and put the smelly food in it. The boy refilled Zero's water bowl from the outside hose. The dog didn't look at the food, but whined and thrust his head against the boy's elbow.

"Better eat," D.J. said softly, giving the mutt a quick pat. But the hair-puller followed D.J. to the end of the chain as the boy walked alongside the porch to feed the hounds.

When D.J. bent to pick up Thunder's pan, Dad yelled through the open screen window. "In the morning, take that hair-puller and try to *give* him away since you can't sell him. Failing that, take him for a walk someplace and lose him!"

D.J. looked down at the little mutt and then bent to rough his head and ears. The boy whispered, "Don't mind him, Zero. Dad's just out of sorts. He doesn't mean that. Still, I guess we'll have to give you away if we can't sell you. But we don't have to do that until tomorrow."

D.J. went on feeding the hounds, wondering why he should care about that little mutt. He was a coward, plain and simple, and he'd caused lots of trouble. D.J. wanted a collie. He didn't want Zero. So why did he feel funny about what happened to that little feist*?

* * * * *

The next morning, D.J. freed Zero's chain from the back porch and called to the little dog. Eagerly, Zero bounded after him down the hill, across the creek and onto the paved county road. But by then, the mutt had sensed something was bothering the boy. Zero quit bouncing around and trotted close to D.J. The chain fell slack in the boy's hand. A car coming toward them slowed and Paul Stagg's big booming voice jerked D.J. out of his deep thoughts.

"Hey, D.J.! Glad I ran into you! Look what I got on the trailer."

D.J. checked the quiet country road for traffic, then crossed with Zero to the shoulder on the other side. "That your bear trap?" D.J. asked.

"That's it!" Paul patted the metal trap with a big hand. "I'm hauling it up to the church camp to get that nuisance bear. What'd you think? Will that trap hold a bear or not?"

The boy and the dog circled the bear trap on the trailer. D.J. figured he could almost stand up straight in the 15-foot-long metal pipe. "Looks strong," he said, patting it with the palm of his hand. It made a booming sound.

Paul Stagg explained, "It's just a big old piece of galvanized culvert made to run under a road and let water pass through it. But it'll work fine for a bear trap because it's so strong no bear can tear it open. And see these bars over both ends? They're steel doors, really. You lift them up by pulleys and set a trigger inside. Both ends of the culvert are left open, with the bars sitting high up in metal tracks. The bear goes in the tunnel after the bait on the trigger. Cat food with a fish base is a good bait. But strawberry jam is the best of all for bears."

"I thought they liked honey best."

"Nothing compares to strawberry jam. Well, when Mr. Bear goes into the trap and touches the bait, both those iron bar doors drop down hard and lock at both ends. No way a bear can get out. Then we use those little wheels to roll the culvert onto a trailer again. After that, we just haul that nuisance bear up to the high country and turn him loose so far away he won't never come back. Want to see how to set the trap? Ride with me up to the church camp. Kathy's already there. Left early this morning with some other families."

D.J. shook his head. "Can't. Dad wants me to see

about getting rid of this worthless ol' dog, even if I
have to give him away."

"Well, like I said before—a dog and a boy deserve
a second chance. But if your father told you to do
something, you'd best do it. Say! I know! Maybe
somebody at the church camp might want your dog!
How about riding along and let's find out?"

Two hours later, D.J. finished touring Cloud's Rest
Church Campground with Paul Stagg. The nuisance
bear had broken into the main dining room kitchen
the night before. D.J. shook his head at how much
damage had been done. The big commercial refrig-
erator had been tipped over and the door ripped off its
hinges. The heavy, thick door of a walk-in freezer
box had also been smashed. Bottles had been broken;
sacks and cans of groceries were tumbled every-
where. Contents of bottles, sacks, and cans were
spilled all over.

Paul picked up a half-gallon can that had held
freestone peaches. "Bear can opener," Paul said
thoughtfully. "Would you believe a bear's claws
could tear up a can like that? Well, I've got to get some
of the men to help me unload this trap. Why don't
you and your dog take a walk around? Maybe you'll
find somebody who'll give your dog a good home.
Or maybe you'll run into my daughter."

The little mutt stayed close to D.J.'s heels as the
boy roamed aimlessly over the rolling and wooded
hills of the church campground. It was an amazing
sight to D.J. to see lots of city kids yelling and playing
and having a good time together. Some rode horses
along trails that wandered in and out of 900 acres of
trees. Others played ball or swam or sat in the shade

and read or made things. Each time D.J. stopped to
ask if anybody wanted a dog, free, they shook their
heads. A couple of boys even laughed and pointed at
the mutt. Zero's ears drooped and he tucked his short
tail tightly against his body. D.J. spoke sharply to the
boys and they apologized. Boy and dog went on. D.J.
didn't see Kathy anyplace.

D.J. and Zero topped a rise and caught a whiff of
the camp garbage dump. Though the camp was two
miles off the paved road, the refuse was hauled away
only once a week. D.J. started to turn away when Zero
woofed. The hackles* went up along his back. He
growled deep in his chest and loudly sniffed at the
grass.

"What is it, Zero? Huh?" D.J. knelt to see for himself and immediately jumped up. "Bear tracks! Fresh
too! The grass is just starting to spring back up
where he trampled it."

The short hairs on the back of D.J.'s neck stood up
in fright as he glanced around. "I don't see anything,
Zero, but let's get out of here!" The little dog needed
no urging. He ran so close to D.J.'s feet that his heels
kept hitting the dog in the lower jaw until D.J. used
the chain to pull the dog to a proper heel position.

When the boy felt safer, he said to the dog, "It's
downright scary, knowing some bears are not afraid of
people. It's especially scary when bears get so bold
they come right into a big campground. I mean, like
this, right in the middle of broad daylight. I sure
wish we'd brought one of the hounds and my rifle.
Well, no sense thinking about that. Let's take one
more walk that way to see if we can find Kathy."

D.J. walked until he found himself in a primitive

area near Jawbone Ridge above Mad River. The brush and rocks were so high and close together the boy was forced to unsnap Zero from his chain to keep him from getting tangled every few feet. Boy and dog were cutting through rough brush and timber when D.J. spotted a dry creek bed. Figuring it'd be easier walking, he scrambled down the hillside and jumped over a log. Then he stopped dead still in his tracks. For the third time that spring, he was looking at a bear!

At once, the boy saw she was a sow. She was a gunnysack blond and maybe weighed 200 pounds. She had not smelled the boy, but she had obviously caught his movement. She woofed uncertainly and raised up on her hind legs like a man. D.J. knew bears didn't see well, but they had a great sense of smell. The wind was from the sow to the boy. The rank smell, something like a wet dog only worse, was strong in the boy's nose. But the boy's only desire was to get away safely.

He started to quietly step back and felt his heels kick Zero in the lower jaw. The little dog yelped in surprise more than pain. Instantly, the bear woofed loudly and clicked her tusks in warning.

D.J. whispered, "Now you've done it, Zero!" The boy saw the sow turn and swipe her forepaw at something. It moved, and for the first time, D.J. saw the cub. It was the same color as its mother. The cub ran a few steps and started climbing the nearest tree. The mother swung her paw and a second cub—a black one—also was spanked up a tree. D.J. started to turn to run when he saw the sow send a brown cub scooting up another tree. *Triplets!*

D.J. knew one of the most dangerous animals is a wild mother bear with young. The boy desperately looked for a safe place. He didn't see any. He glanced back. With all three cubs safely scooting up different trees, the bear started toward D.J. and the dog.

No sense being quiet now. D.J. yelled, "Run, Zero! Run!"

Boy and dog ran until D.J.'s lungs seemed on fire and he had a stitch in his side. Then D.J. dared to steal a glance over his shoulder. The bear was still in place, the triplets following her around.

"Boy!" D.J. said, flopping down on the hillside to catch his breath, "we ran a lot farther than we needed to! But I wasn't about to look back and see if she was gaining on us. Let's rest and see what she does."

The sow is amazingly like a person, D.J. thought. When danger threatened, her first concern had been for her young. Like a human mother, when her little ones were safe, she turned to face whatever danger there was. When the danger passed, she went back to her motherly duties. D.J. watched the cubs tumbling and playing like puppies.

"You know what, Zero?" D.J. whispered. "If I can't have a collie, maybe I could have a cub. Didn't Paul Stagg say he once had a bear cub? I think he did! I'll have to ask him about that."

Zero wagged his tail and whined softly. He laid his muzzle on D.J.'s cork-soled boots. D.J. glanced down at the mutt, then lifted his eyes to watch the bears. They were still in the open area.

Suddenly, the boy caught a flash of red moving upwind toward the bears. D.J. leaped to his feet.

"That's a girl! She's going to run right into—"

A scream interrupted. The terror in the voice turned D.J.'s whole body to goosebumps. For a moment, D.J. stood uncertainly. Then the scream came again. He caught another flickering glimpse of the girl. She'd apparently tripped and fallen. She was scrambling backward on hands and knees, screaming. She turned and D.J. saw her face.

His voice exploded in the mountain stillness, "Kathy!"

He started running down the hill, shouting so his throat ached with the power of his cry. He didn't know what he was going to do, but he had to do something. He reached the clearing where he had first seen the sow. The cubs had apparently again been spanked up a tree. Kathy had scrambled up on a huge granite boulder. The bear was pacing around the bottom. D.J. wasn't sure if she couldn't climb the smooth boulder or if she didn't want to. The boy slid to a halt just beyond a fallen log. "Kathy, you OK?" he called, gasping for breath.

"Yes . . . I . . . I think so."

The bear heard D.J. and swung her big head to look at him. She woofed a warning. He tried to think what to do. But before he could make a decision, he heard Zero bark. Instantly, the bear clicked her teeth and charged!

Kathy shrieked, "Run, D.J., run!"

Chapter Eight

SILENCE FOR A HAIR-PULLING HERO

D.J. ran away from the bear, frantically looking for safety. He heard the mad mother bear's clicking tusks behind him. He heard her warning huffing sounds: *Uf! Uf! Uf!* Out of the corner of his eye, D.J. saw Zero crouched under the fallen log.

D.J.'s eyes lifted. Beside the log was a half-grown tree with one limb sticking straight out. Even though he knew the bear could easily climb a tree, D.J. saw no other choice. He jumped up on the log, crouched to give his legs more spring, then leaped. His arms stretched to their limits. His fingers curled around the limb. The boy threw his feet against the tree trunk to swing onto the limb. His weight was too much! The limb snapped off and the boy fell heavily.

He twisted his body to land on the far side of the fallen log. Out of the corner of his eye, he saw the sow stop to check her cubs. D.J. landed hard on his hands and knees just beyond the log. Bright flecks of light flickered before his eyes. His breath was knocked out. But he heard Kathy yell, "Look out! She's after you again!"

D.J. leaped up, ignoring the bruises and pains in his hands and knees. He caught a glimpse of the bear charging toward him, knocking down saplings and bursting through brush as if they didn't exist.

The boy saw only one other hope of safety. Another boulder, bigger than Kathy's, rose out of the tangle of brush and vines. It was on the other side of the log, nearer the bear and Kathy. Then the bear was upon him, her huge blond forepaws reaching across the fallen log. The big mouth opened and the terrible clicking teeth were inches away. D.J. threw up his left arm to protect his face.

Zero shot from under the log like a greased pig out of a cannon. The little mutt's incredibly loud bark sounded once, challenging and sharp. D.J. saw the dog streak toward the bear, leap high, and grab at the bear's short tail.

With a roar that shook the trees and echoed off the canyon walls, the sow spun away from D.J. and snapped at the dog. But Zero dashed away, his hindquarter tucked under him so he almost seemed to be sitting down while running. The mutt's stub tail almost scrubbed against the ground. Sharp, loud barks exploded like machine-gun fire. Zero ran in a wide circle, dodging in and out of brush. The bear smashed through like a man hoeing down weeds.

D.J. yelled, "Keep running, Zero! Run! Run!"

Zero kept barking and dodging. The bear stopped and turned back, but the little hair-puller was upon her instantly. He leaped up and grabbed her

right hip, growling through the mouthful of hair.
The sow spun to smash the dog with immense forepaws, but Zero leaped away. He crouched, forefeet
to the ground, backside sticking up in the air, his sharp
bark goading the bear. When she spurted after him,
Zero turned and zipped away, barking rapidly.

Kathy yelled something, but D.J.'s mind was too
busy to register her words. He made a decision. When
Zero led the mad sow to the farthest point of a cirle,
out of sight behind the brush and boulders, the boy
moved.

He bent low and ran rapidly across the open area
of dry wash toward the second big boulder he'd seen.
D.J. judged the easiest way up the slick monolith.*
He used hands and knees to scramble up to safety.

He reached the highest and most level spot and
turned to look below. Zero charged out of the brush
into the open, joyfully barking, the bear huffing behind like a fat man shoveling snow. The dog dashed
toward D.J.'s boulder.

"Oh, no!" he moaned. "Don't bring her here!"

D.J. felt goosebumps leap up over his head and
shoulders as the bear broke off chasing the dog and
stopped at the bottom of his boulder. She sniffed
where D.J. had crawled up. She placed big paws with
terrible-looking claws on the boulder as though she
would try climbing up after the boy.

Kathy yelled, "Look out!" But it wasn't necessary.
D.J. was doing all he could to pull his knees under his
chin and sit as small as possible.

Zero dashed around the far side of the boulder,
saw the bear, and charged toward her. The bear took
up the chase again, then stopped.

D.J. was horrified to see the sow shuffle toward Kathy's rock. The little hair-puller chased after the bear, barking, leaping up to grab a mouthful of bear leg or hair, but the sow kept going toward Kathy.

When the bear stopped and put a forepaw on Kathy's boulder, ignoring the dog, D.J. yelled.

"Hey, Bear! Look at me! I'm coming down!" The boy slid down the boulder, skinning his hands. He landed on his feet and stamped his feet hard, like he was running in place. The bear seemed to turn inside her loose hide. She charged the boy.

D.J. scrambled up the boulder again on hands and knees. He was almost at the top when he slipped and fell flat against the smooth monolith. He started sliding down as fast as on ice.

He heard Kathy scream, then Zero bark and growl. The bear roared as D.J. regained his hands and knees and skittered up the boulder. In a second, he'd reached the top and turned around. The bear was threatening him at the bottom of the boulder. Zero was leaping in and out, dodging the bear's jaws and claws.

D.J. yelled, "Be careful, Zero! Watch out!" The little dog took that as a word of encouragement. He leaped high, caught the bear right on the end of her short tail. The sow roared and spun around to swat her tormentor, but the little dog was racing away. The bear chased him.

The boy swallowed hard, checked to see that he wasn't seriously injured from his face-first slide down the boulder, and made a decision. He looked across the clearing at the second boulder. "Kathy, can you slide down the far side of your rock?"

She turned her head to check, then looked back at D.J. She called, "I . . . I think so."

"When Zero's led that bear away again, you slide down that rock and get out of here. Stay out of sight, keeping the boulder between you and the bear."

"What about you?"

"Your dad's at the church campground. Tell him where I am."

"Will you be OK?"

"I will as long as Zero doesn't get caught! Ready? Go! Go!"

Two hours later, D.J. began to be uneasy. Kathy hadn't returned. No matter how the boy strained to hear, there were no sounds of rescue. The boy cast anxious glances toward the hillside that rose sharply beside him. Had Kathy gotten lost? Maybe she'd been hurt on the way out and had not yet reached her father. Maybe she couldn't find her way back. Maybe. . . .

D.J. told himself fiercely, *Stop it! No sense scaring myself like that. I've got to think what to do in case Kathy doesn't bring help.*

Then the boy saw another problem. Zero was definitely slowing up. Every time he ran panting, tongue rolling, the bear was closer. *Unless something is done soon,* D.J. thought, *the bear will kill Zero.*

He thought about praying. But he hadn't done that since his mother was dying. His prayers hadn't done any good then. Why would they be any good now?

Take Zero up with him? That would be the only way. But the dog was stocky and heavy even though he wasn't very big. Could D.J. pick up Zero, and climb that slick boulder with the dog in his arms? Or would boy and dog slide right into the bear's terrible teeth and claws?

"I don't see what else to do," D.J. said aloud. "When Zero comes back around again, I'll try it."

He drew himself together, muscles tight, ready to act. His mind screamed warnings. He'd heard what terrible things happened where someone stumbled upon a sow with young. Yet, as the sun started sliding toward the western mountains and shadows crept into the canyon, D.J. had new respect for the blond sow.

She was a good mother. Periodically, she sniffed at the base of the different trees. The little dog, apparently glad for the rest, sat down on his haunches out of reach and panted heavily. When the sow was satisfied that all three cubs were safe, she checked Kathy's boulder. The bear circled the monolith and seemed to know the girl had escaped. For a moment, D.J.'s heart seemed to stop as the bear sniffed loudly behind Kathy's boulder and followed her scent a few feet into the brush.

D.J. yelled. "Hey, you! Bear! Look! I'm coming down! Come get me!" He made a motion as though he was going to slide down the huge boulder again. The bear ignored him.

For the second time, D.J. slid down from his boulder. He ran toward the bear, shouting and waving his arms. The sow spun back toward him. D.J. streaked for his boulder, hearing Zero's attack bark and the bear's snapping teeth.

The boy turned around in time to see the bear suddenly double back on her own body and almost catch the little mutt. Zero raced away, the bear almost upon him.

"Oh, no!" D.J. exclaimed. "She's getting closer
and closer!"

Dog and bear crashed through the brush and out
of sight again. D.J. made up his mind.

"When they come around again, I'll jump down
and get him unless she's too close."

For the second time, he tensed himself to act. Suddenly, D.J. heard a sound like a bird whistling. It
wasn't a bird he recognized. He also heard the sow
stop her chase. A moment later, she reappeared in the
clearing.

What had made the bear break off her chase
when she was so close to catching her tormentor? D.J.
watched as she stopped at the base of a bull pine.*
She reared up on her hind legs and placed her powerful forepaws on the tree trunk. She sniffed loudly,
her long neck extended toward the lower limbs of the
tree. Zero flopped down heavily about 30 feet away
and watched the bear.

D.J. heard the sound again. It came from the tree.
The boy strained his eyes. Slowly, he made out the
shape of the black cub. It opened its mouth and the
birdlike sound came again.

"Well, how about that?" D.J. asked softly aloud.
"It's the cub doing that! Guess he's complaining about
having to stay up there so long!"

The boy wished Zero hadn't suddenly turned from
being a coward to a hero who single-handedly took on
that mad mother bear. But how much longer could
the little mutt last? The bear had repeatedly charged
through mountain and black oak, buck brush, and
wild choke cherries. She had gone through them like a

hot knife through freshly-churned butter. Zero had been forced to go around. He had run a lot farther than she had, and that was part of the reason the chase was beginning to go her way.

The cub started to back down the tree, but the mother made a warning sound. The cub reversed directions and climbed rapidly back out of sight in the branches.

D.J. laughed in spite of himself. Instantly, he wished he hadn't. The sow dropped down on all fours and came lumbering toward him. D.J. looked around for some way of defending himself, but there was none.

He watched her approach while his neck, shoulders, and arms rippled with gooseflesh. D.J. knew she could have climbed a tree if he'd taken one. He shivered, glad he hadn't. But now D.J. wasn't sure a bear couldn't climb a boulder, though he'd never heard of such a thing. The mother bear circled the monolith, looking up at the boy. When she got around in back of D.J.'s perch, she stood on her hind legs. She leaned her left forepaw against the slick side of granite and thrust the other forepaw up above her head.

D.J. drew up his feet until his knees were under his chin. He wrapped his arms about his legs and made himself as small as possible. He watched in terror as the sow's hooked, ugly claws inched closer to his feet. He drew back until he was in danger of falling over backward. When the bear's right front claw touched his boot sole, D.J. raised his foot slightly and kicked at the forepaw. At the same time, he screeched in panic.

That was Zero's cue. He barked sharply, leaped to

his feet and charged the bear again. She ignored him, still reaching for the boy. Out of the corner of his eye, D.J. saw the little heeler rush within a few feet of the bear. The dog stopped, barked, and half-turned, ready to race away again when the bear gave chase. But she didn't seem to notice the dog as she kept reaching for D.J.

The boy saw the long, shaggy forearm straining toward him again. He smelled the bear's rank, unpleasant odor. D.J. let out a shriek of pure fright.

Instantly, the dog rushed in, leaped high and grabbed a mouthful of bear hair. The sow roared, dropped to all fours and thrust out her long neck with terrible jaws open to crush the mutt.

Zero barked and dashed away, but this time the bear was just a half-jump behind. Zero zipped through the underbrush. The bear smashed over them. Dog and bear disappeared behind a smaller boulder.

D.J. heard the bear's tusks clicking and the short puffing sounds. Then D.J. heard something else too!

Zero yelped just once.

D.J. heard the chase stop. There was no more brush being smashed. There was no more clicking of bear teeth and no more huffing.

Worst of all, there was no barking!

D.J. stood up quickly on the boulder. "Zero? Hey, Zero! Zero!"

The words bounced off both sides of the canyon wall. But there was no joyful answering bark from the little mutt.

A moment later, the bear came slowly back into view. Her jaws were red with fresh blood.

"Oh, no! Zero! Here, Zero! Come here, Boy!"

There was no answer. There was no sound of movement in the brush. All D.J. saw was the bear ambling slowly across the dry wash, her terrible jaws bright red. She ignored him and went to check the trees with her cubs.

D.J. called again. "Zero! Zero!" D.J. yelled so loudly his throat hurt. He listened. But when his words had echoed into silence up the canyon, there was only a terrible, terrible silence. There wasn't a sound from the little hair-pulling bear dog.

D.J.'s knees melted and he slowly sank down on the boulder. He buried his face in his hands. Tears came fast.

Chapter Nine

MEMORIAL FOR A HERO

When darkness came, D.J. was hoarse from calling for the little dog. The boy's eyes felt swollen. He was sick and hurt inside. The sow had still been waiting for him at dusk. He wasn't sure if she was still out there or not. He huddled on top of the boulder, cold and miserable, aching for Zero and wondering what had happened to Kathy.

Suddenly, the boy sat up, straining to hear. In a moment, it came again. "Deeee Jaaay!"

Paul Stagg! There was no mistaking that giant's rumbling voice. The boy cupped his hands about his mouth and yelled, "Over here!"

The big lay preacher, Kathy, and several armed men with flashlights soon arrived. The mother bear had gone. Paul helped D.J. down. They treated his cuts and scratches, covered him with a leather jacket while some searched for the little dog's body. Kathy explained she'd taken a wrong turn. That's why she was so long getting back. D.J. told her it was OK. He watched as searching flashlights stopped where he had pointed out the last time he'd seen Zero.

Someone called through the night. "We found where it happened. But the body's not here. Most likely crawled off somewhere to die."

D.J. felt a brief surge of hope, then he realized the truth. A coyote or other animal had carried off the little dog's body. Aloud, D.J. said, "I'm coming back here to hunt for him in the daylight."

Paul's deep rumbling voice answered. "I'll come with you, D.J. Now, let's get you home."

* * * * *

D.J. slept until almost noon. He was awakened by his father. "The newspaper editor from that weekly at the county seat is here. He wants to take your picture and talk to you."

D.J. slid into his pants and came into the living room. The boy had never been interviewed by a newspaper reporter. He answered questions about how it happened, ending with the dog's last yelp. By then, he was trying hard not to let tears come.

The reporter stopped writing. "You're quite a hero, D.J. Dillon, and so is—was—your little dog. What'd you say his name was? Zero?"

D.J. hesitated, then said fiercely, "I hate that name! Don't call him that!"

Grandpa tapped his shillelagh on the pine floor. "Mr. Newspaperman, you didn't hear the straight of that name. The dog's name was Hero."

When the reporter had gone, D.J. looked across the table at his father. His sore leg was sticking out straight on the bench.

"Dad, I'm going after that outlaw bear."

"I can't let you do that!"

"On the way home last night, Paul told me he'd go with me. But he's only got a week, then he's got to go somewhere else to preach for a while."

"You mean he's moving away? His whole family?"

"Guess so. But Kathy doesn't want to go. She said she's tired of moving and hopes they can stay here until she's through high school, at least. Her father said he'd like to, but he's got to go where the Gospel's not being preached, and that means Sheet Iron Mountain next."

Dad snapped, "Then we'd be without a preacher at Stoney Ridge."

D.J. blinked. Had his father said *we?*

Dad lowered his eyes. "D.J., when they brought word yesterday what had happened, and where you were, I thought maybe—I was afraid—well, I. . . ."

Dad's voice trailed into silence. D.J. frowned, unsure of what his father was trying to say.

Finally Dad spoke again, very quietly. "Son, if you was to want to go to church Sunday, well, uh, that is— I'd go with you."

D.J. stared. Dad wouldn't even go to church with Mom when she was alive. D.J. asked, "Grandpa too?"

"It was his idea."

* * * * *

That Sunday morning as D.J., Dad, and Grandpa were driving down the short main street of Stoney Ridge, the boy saw a familiar black pickup parked against the high curb.

Dad recognized it at the same time. He hit the brake pedal. "I owe Abst something!" he cried. Dad cut sharply to park behind the black pickup.

Grandpa said softly, "Not today, Sam! Not today."

Dad hesitated. The Absts walked out of the town's only mercantile store. D.J. saw the professional bear hunter and his son look at the Dillons a moment. Nails started to sneer, but his father sharply nudged him in the ribs. Mr. Abst nodded ever so slightly toward the Dillons.

Grandpa said softly, "Well, would you look at that? D.J., they must'a read about what you done in the newspaper."

Grandpa nodded back. In another second, Dad did the same. So did D.J. Dad let out the clutch. "It's nice," he said, "but that won't stop them from trying to beat you and Paul to that outlaw bear."

"We'll beat them," D.J. said firmly. "Those Absts been chasing that bear for weeks without any luck. Now it's our turn."

Grandpa shook his head. "You won't have much time either way. The Absts will either beat you to the bear, or the preacher will move away, and you won't be able to hunt that bear without the preacher."

"We'll beat the Absts," D.J. repeated as Dad turned into the church parking lot. "And we're going to do it with a trap!" Before his father could protest too much, people swarmed over to them and started congratulating D.J. and everyone talked at once.

D.J. had never seen the little church so full. Maybe that was because Paul Stagg had visited the Dillon home on Wednesday and learned they were coming to church. There had been just time for a sidebar in the local newspaper alongside the story about the rescue. Usually, D.J. would have been so proud he could

have burst, but today he was sad because of losing
his little dog.

After the opening prayer and a hymn, Paul Stagg
stood to make the announcements and then introduce
visitors. "We have some very distinguished people
with us today, as I'm sure you've noticed. Since you've
all read the papers or talked to my daughter about
what happened, I'll just skip that and introduce everyone. First, the grandfather and father of our local
hero. Caleb and Sam Dillon, please stand so everyone
can see you."

Grandpa and Dad stood quickly and sat right
down. Then Paul Stagg asked D.J. to stand. Slowly, he
got to his feet. Paul began the applause. It swept the
congregation. But they did more than clap. All the people stood up, applauding louder and louder.

D.J.'s neck felt hot. He lowered his eyes, but out of
the corner of them he could see Kathy smiling at him.
Mrs. Higgins looked as though she was going to
burst with pride. Even little Priscilla Higgins was
standing, applauding, her eyes serious. He'd never
seen such a look from her before. The clapping finally
faded away and people sat down. D.J. did the same,
feeling his face and neck so hot it seemed his shirt
would scorch.

The preacher said softly, "Of course, you folks
know that neither my daughter nor D.J. Dillon might
be here today if it weren't for a little hair-pulling
bear dog. Now, I'm not an ordained minister and I've
had no regular schooling in such things, but I love
the Lord and all He made. That includes dogs."

Paul Stagg paused, then said, "Since I'm a hound
dog man from away back, it seems to me it would be a

right thing to have a moment of silence. You might
want to think about what it means to love someone so
much you'd give up your life for the one you love.
Jesus did that for us, and that little hair-pulling dog did
it for D.J. Dillon and for my daughter."

The church was very, very still. D.J. fought tears
that scalded the back of his eyelids. Grandpa sniffed
and Dad rubbed his forefinger against the corner of
his right eye.

The lay pastor ended the moment of silence by
starting a hymn. The pianist picked it up and the people joined in.

When it was time for the sermon, Paul Stagg stood
and said, "Today I'm going to talk about Joseph in the
Old Testament. Since that story covers several chap-
ters in Genesis, I'm going to just tell you briefly what
happened before I get to the point I want to make."

Paul Stagg told about teenage Joseph being sold
into slavery by his brothers. Joseph was falsely accused
of a crime and put in prison for a long time. When
he was finally released, he became the second most important man in Egypt, next only to the pharaoh or
king of that country. Eventually, when food was scarce
in Joseph's native land, his brothers came down to
Egypt where there was food which Joseph had saved
for the people.

The brothers didn't recognize Joseph, but by and
by he told them who he was. They were afraid Joseph
would hurt them because they had sold him into
slavery.

"Now," the big lay preacher said in a voice that
shook the little church's rafters, "notice what Joseph
says in Genesis 50:20. Joseph says to his brothers,

'You meant evil against me, but God meant it for good in order to bring about this present result.' "

Paul Stagg closed his Bible on the pulpit and walked around to the side of it. "Here's the point, folks: You can't always help what happens to you. You can't help where you were born, or maybe the place where you live, or the conditions.

"But you *can* control your reaction; how you feel and act toward those conditions. That's called your 'attitude.' You have a choice about that. You should keep a good one because things aren't always what they seem."

D.J. couldn't explain it, but instantly he knew some things as surely as if someone had told him. Grandpa was cranky and always arguing with Dad because the old man hurt. He hurt like that outlaw bear that had turned mean. Dad hurt because his wife had died and he had a young son to raise alone. Dad hurt because his leg was injured and he couldn't work and the bills were piling up. Yet none of that had seemed that way until a second ago.

And Zero—Hero—had run away from his first bear fight. Yet the little dog wasn't really a coward. He loved D.J. enough that the little hair-puller had challenged that mad mother bear. The dog had saved both Kathy's and D.J.'s lives at the cost of his own life. It hadn't seemed he was brave enough to do that.

Yet D.J. didn't understand some things. How could anything good come out of his mother dying, or his father and grandfather arguing, or the little dog getting killed?

The boy heard the lay preacher's words again. "The Scriptures tell us that man looks on the outside, but God looks on the inside, on the heart. Man looks at his problems. He looks at his surroundings and his losses and his pains and he feels sorry for himself.

"But God looks on things that are going to be because He knows what's down the road for us. He knows we've got to go through these things we don't like to get us ready for what is coming. And someday, like Joseph, we can look back and say, 'It wasn't people or circumstances that sent me here, but God!' "

D.J. stole a glance at his father and grandfather. Their eyes were lowered. The boy wondered what they were thinking.

The big lay preacher began to wind up his sermon. "But sometimes we need help to deal with things. We need help to be changed from the inside so we can live like Joseph. If you'd like the Lord to help you, no matter what your problem, come down here to the front of this church and get it done!"

D.J. closed his eyes. He ached for the little hair-puller. He'd rather have him back alive than any collie dog.

D.J. thought about going to the front of the church. *What would Dad and Grandpa say? What would the kids at school say? Especially, what would Nails Abst say?*

Grandpa whispered, "D.J., I'm a'going to walk down there. You want to come with me?"

D.J. hesitated. In all his life, he'd never expected his grandfather to do anything like that. What had happened to him? Why had he and Dad even come to church?

Grandpa whispered, "Sam, you want to come too?"

Dad shook his head. "Not this time. But you and D.J. go ahead if you want."

The congregation was singing the last verse. Grandpa stood up. "You coming, D.J.?"

Chapter Ten

RACE TO CAPTURE THE OUTLAW BEAR

When church was over, it seemed everyone surrounded the Dillon family. D.J. wanted to escape all the attention, but he was trapped. Mrs. Higgins hurried over with Priscilla right behind her. The widow shook Grandpa's hand. She said cheerfully, "You just made the wisest decision in your life, Mr. Dillon."

Grandpa leaned on his Irish shillelagh and nodded soberly. "There comes a time to set things in order."

Pris eased up to D.J. He watched her carefully. Even in church, he wasn't sure he could trust her. She said, "I'm sorry about your little dog, D.J."

The boy didn't know what to say. He just nodded.

Grandpa spoke up. "Things like that come to all of us, sooner or later. We've got to deal with them."

Mrs. Higgins nodded. "True, but that doesn't make it any easier. Sam, will you and your family join Pris and me for something to eat? I've invited Brother Paul and his family too."

D.J. looked up at his father. He rubbed his cleanly shaven chin. "Hannah, I've been thinking we should talk, but we can't with so many people around."

"Oh." Mrs. Higgins sounded disappointed. "Well, all right." She smiled at D.J. "For a minute awhile ago, I thought you were going to go forward with your grandfather."

"Maybe some other time," D.J. answered, looking at the worn wooden floor.

"Sam, I know you don't hold much with such things, but since you came to church today—"

"We'll talk about it later, Hannah."

Mrs. Higgins looked at Dad for a long moment. Then she smiled and turned to look down at D.J. "You know it's not necessary to be in church to make a decision for the Lord. It can be any time, any place."

"I know," D.J. answered, lowering his eyes, "my mother taught me."

"Oh." Mrs. Higgins' voice seemed small and faint. She glanced at Dad. D.J. saw some kind of look pass between them.

Other people crowded around, shaking Grandpa's hand, saying things to Dad and trying to rumple the boy's hair. He slipped away and out the side door into the warm July sunshine. He heard someone following and turned, ready to defend himself against Pris. But it was Kathy who stood before him.

"My father says you and he got to talk."

"About going after that outlaw bear, I expect."

"Probably. Word came just before we left the house that they'd caught that nuisance bear raiding the church camp. They'll truck him up to the high country and bring the trap back. You and Dad can use it."

"Thanks. I'll talk to him soon's he gets through shaking hands with everybody."

Kathy's blue eyes focused upon his face. She looked very somber. "You were awful brave back with that mother bear."

"My dog was brave; not me."

"You were *both* brave."

Pris came out the side door and called. "D.J., Brother Paul's asking for you."

The boy raised his voice. "I'll be right there."

Only Dad and Grandpa remained at the front door to shake hands with the lay preacher. Everyone else had filed by and were spread out under the ponderosa trees talking in small groups. As D.J., Kathy, and Pris approached, Dad reached his right hand out to the big man.

"Paul, I guess you know I came here today to sort of say 'thanks' for protecting my son and your girl from that bear. First time I've been inside a church in many a year."

D.J. wondered why Dad had come to church to thank Paul Stagg when he had been at the house earlier this week. Then the boy understood. Dad hadn't come to thank any man. D.J.'s eyes opened wide in surprise. He'd never guessed Dad had any soft feelings about Jesus.

Dad still held the big man's hand. Dad said, "Paul, I thought I'd lost my boy once this week. He's about all I got left. I'm not anxious to worry about him again, but I understand you're willing to help him go after that outlaw bear?"

"D.J. and I are going to try our best."

"You know that Abst fellow and his son are running that bear practically every day?"

Paul Stagg's hearty laughter echoed back from the now empty church. "It's the *end* of a race that counts, Sam! D.J. and I've got a good chance."

Dad asked, "How so?"

"You know that Lum Yee who owns the mercantile store? Well, everybody tells him things. And he tells me that all the hunters—including Abst— always lose that outlaw in the same general area. That's in Devil's Slide Canyon where Mad River runs through it. I've hunted that country in years gone by, and I think I know something that will give us a mite of an edge in trapping that bear!"

Dad said, "I just learned about that trap idea as we were parking the truck. Are you serious, Paul?"

The giant's voice rumbled from deep in his big chest. "Sam, don't worry about it! I've worked those kinds of traps before. Besides, we'll carry heavy caliber rifles as backup. And I promise you I'll take as good care of D.J. as if he were my own kin."

Dad pursed his lips, then said quietly, "Paul, you went into that canyon at night to bring out my son. I thank you for that. Guess I'll trust you with him again if he wants to go trapping that outlaw bear with you."

D.J. felt all eyes turn to him. "I want to go, Dad. Long's I get to look for my dog on the way."

Grandpa cackled and pounded his walking cane on the church step. "Going to be a real horse race with that Abst fellow and his boy! I hear tell they think they'll get that bear for sure in the next few days."

D.J. said, "We'll beat them, won't we, Paul?"

Paul laughed. "If the good Lord's with us and the crick* don't rise! But we won't have much time because I'm leaving in a week to see about helping another church on Sheet Iron Mountain where they need a preacher."

Dad shook his head. "Paul, it sure beats me how you can leave this here church when it don't have a replacement for you."

"I've trained some good lay leaders during the time I've been here, Sam. Hannah, here, is a mighty strong Bible student. Got several men who can take hold and hang on too. But that church at Sheet Iron Mountain doesn't have any leadership. Hasn't had for over a year. They asked me to come."

Dad frowned. "You so all-fired bound and determined to go that you won't entertain a notion of changing your mind and staying here?"

The giant's laughter was pleasant to D.J.'s ears. "Sam," the preacher said, "if anything happens to make me change my mind, I'd be the first one to stay here and let down roots clean through to China. But as it now stands, I got just one week to get that bear with your son."

On the drive home, there was a strange silence in the cab of Dad's pickup. D.J. was wedged between his father and grandfather. It was so crowded in the single seat that usually Dad and Grandpa would have been quarrelsome. But not today. D.J. wondered if it had anything to do with Grandpa making a decision to live for Jesus. The grandfather seemed to read D.J.'s mind. As the pickup growled up a steep hill lined with beautiful conifers, the old man cleared his throat.

"D.J., I 'spect you're a'wonderin' why I done what I done this morning?"

The boy nodded, looking up at his grandfather. The old man's blue eyes were looking into the distance, past the trees to white thunderheads boiling up over the higher Sierras.

Grandpa said softly, "About 50 years ago, I hit the sawdust trail, as they used to call it back then. I stayed on it for a while. Then I backslid. But lately I've been thinking about a lot of things. I sorta figured I'd been wrong all these years. So I did what was right."

D.J. frowned. "What made you change your mind?"

His father nudged D.J. in the ribs. "Don't ask such questions! Just listen."

D.J.'s question seemed perfectly logical to him. He looked at both men and waited until Grandpa spoke again.

The old man's eyes misted as he took the boy's hand in his. D.J. was surprised to feel how thin it was, and how it seemed to shake as with the cold even though it was now July.

"Wasted my life, D.J., mostly, I did. Like Samson in the Bible. He was born in answer to his parents' prayer, born to do something special. But Samson went through life doing his own thing, as they say. God never interferes with a man's right to choose, even if it's wrong and not what God wants. But Samson faced death before he prayed again. Did you know I had a praying ma, same as you did?"

D.J. shook his head.

Grandpa continued. "Your great-grandma Dillon was a powerful praying woman! She used to pray something fierce for me and your dad, back when he was growing up."

The boy glanced at his father. Dad had never once said anything about such things.

Grandpa spoke again. "Your dad used to go to church some. I never went, but sometimes I thought about it. Guess a praying woman's prayers stay with you. I reckon my wife musta prayed all of 30 years for what I done today. And your mother, D.J., well, she prayed for all of us: me, your father, and you. I sure hope they know part of their prayers are finally answered."

Dad had been very quiet. "Seems like that everything's changing since that Paul Stagg come to town."

Grandpa chuckled. "The widder woman's always been a God-fearing person, I reckon. She's just come back to what was important to her. Her faith. But I reckon you and she will have to work that out between yourselves, now, Sam. My guess is she won't have ye unlessen ye get right with—"

"Enough!" Dad's voice exploded in the small truck cab.

D.J. suddenly remembered what Pris had once said about her mother marrying Dad. The boy asked, "Dad, you ever going to get married again?"

Dad drove in silence a moment. "Would that bother you if I did, Son?"

D.J. looked up in surprise. His father hadn't called him "Son" in a long, long time. D.J. thought a minute before answering. "Nobody can take Mom's place."

"No," Dad agreed, "I didn't mean that."

Grandpa added, "What you father means is that nobody can replace another person like a wife that's died. But the living get lonesome and they need somebody. God said, 'It's not good for man to be alone.' And in the Bible, Abraham remarried when he was old and his wife died, and—"

"Dad's not Abraham!" D.J. spoke with some warmth. The idea of another woman in Dad's life bothered him, especially when he realized who Dad was thinking about. And Pris—she'd be a terrible stepsister! The boy added, "Besides, *you* didn't remarry, Grandpa!"

"I've studied on it some these last few years since your grandmother passed on, D.J. But your dad's still a young man—"

Dad interrupted. "I think D.J. has heard all he wants about that subject." Dad slowed the pickup to cross the creek below their house. "I just asked what you felt, Son, and I understand. Let's forget it."

D.J. didn't answer. He understood in a vague way that Dad had a right to remarry, and Mrs. Higgins was the person he was thinking about. And she was thinking about Dad the same way. D.J. dropped his head suddenly and put his hand on his forehead.

Dad said firmly, "We're almost home. I'll help you get ready to go hunting with Paul so you two can catch that outlaw bear."

The boy brightened. "It's going to be some chase, Dad! Maybe something I'll never forget!"

D.J. didn't know how right he was.

Chapter Eleven

OL' SATCHEL FOOT OUTSMARTS D.J.

The next day, D.J. and the lay preacher bounced along an old logging road toward the bottom of Devil's Slide Canyon. During the long, slow drive in a borrowed gray pickup with the culvert trap on a trailer behind the dog box, D.J. told Paul Stagg about his father's question on remarriage.

The giant's voice rumbled in the dusty cab. "You're against your father remarrying, D.J.?"

"I've been thinking about that. I don't want somebody to take Mom's place, and yet I know Dad's lonely. But maybe it'll be better now that Grandpa's become a Christian. Do you know he took out his fiddle last night and played? I sang with him even if I do sound like a tromped-on toadfrog, as Grandpa says. It was almost like before Mom died."

The big man laughed. "What'd your dad do?"

"He just kept looking at me, but not saying anything. Seemed to be thinking."

112

"D.J., some day your father probably will get married again. He's got that right, and he should. But I'm sure he'd want you to approve too. Can you?"

"I don't think so, at least, not now."

They drove on, the fine dust feeling like sandpaper between their teeth. They spent some time checking the area where the sow had caught up with the heroic little dog. At last Paul Stagg stopped, removed his cowboy hat, and wiped his brow.

"D.J., we've looked and called until my eyes hurt and my voice is hoarse. If that hair-puller is still alive, he's no place close enough to hear us."

D.J. sat down on the fallen log where he'd tangled with the mad mother bear nearly two weeks before. "You think there's any chance my dog's OK?"

The giant's voice was gentle, but it still rumbled with a powerful feeling. "I got to be honest, D.J. No, I don't think that's likely."

"But there's a chance?"

"Long's nobody's seen his body or brought in his dog collar, there's a chance, I suppose. But not hardly likely."

Slowly, D.J. sighed. "I just can't give up hoping," he said. "I just can't."

"Hope's what keeps us going sometimes, D.J. Well, if we're going to get that trap set before dark, we'd best be a'going."

The afternoon sun was already sliding fast toward the western canyon walls when D.J. watched Paul Stagg carefully crawl backward out of the culvert trap. The smell of cat food bait with a fish-oil base made D.J. wrinkle his nose.

The giant stood and said, "There! It's all set for Ol'

Satchel Foot. You got that strawberry jam smeared around the area?"

"All smeared," D.J. said cheerfully.

Paul rubbed his hands on an old gunny sack to try removing some of the bait smell. D.J. again wrinkled his nose and turned to survey the area. "You pretty sure this is the best place for that trap?"

"Best we can do with just one trap, D.J. Near's I could make out from what Mr. Yee told me Tinsley Abst had said to him, this is that bear's home territory."

"But it's practically on this old logging road. It's less than two miles off the paved county road, and maybe a mile to the hermit's place, if I've got my bearings right."

"You've got that right, D.J. But we're also right in the bottom of Devil's Slide Canyon. Straight up on both sides, as you can see." The big man pointed. "Off over that stand of prime timber is Jawbone Peak where Mad River gets started from melting snows collected in hundreds of little creeks."

The lay preacher's big hand moved on, drawing D.J.'s eyes with it. Paul continued, "The riverbed's so narrow through the canyon that the snow water gets moving pretty fast. That's where it got it's name of 'mad,' meaning, 'like crazy.' Wouldn't do for a man to fall in it above those little falls there. But just below them a half mile or so where we're a'standing, the stream bed widens out considerable, so the water slows up some. In fact, right below the trap it's shallow enough to wade if you're careful."

D.J. asked, "So that's why Ol' Satchel Foot calls this his home territory?"

"Right you are, D.J.! It's close enough to civiliza-
tion for that sick bear to get easy man-food. Yet it's also
remote and primitive enough with these high canyon
walls, heavy timber, and brush. So he's got privacy too.
My guess is that's why the Absts or no other hunter
has been able to take him. He gives them the slip here
in his own backyard."

"Think we'll get him?" D.J. asked, studying the
iron bar doors poised above both ends of the sturdy
metal culvert.

"We will if that bear gets a whiff of that strawberry jam you put out, or if'n he smells this fish-oil base."

"And if Mr. Abst doesn't kill the bear first."

"Got to take that chance, D.J. Well, it'll be dark if
we don't leave now and try that hermit's place again.
We got to see if he'll loan us his hair-puller, even as
old as he is."

*　*　*　*　*

Mr. Zeering came to the door holding a kerosene
lantern high until he recognized D.J. He introduced
Paul Stagg who shook hands with the hermit. Then
Mr. Zeering turned to the boy.

"I've been expecting you. Most likely you're
a'looking for that there little mutt of yores?"

D.J. blinked in surprise. "My dog?"

"Same one you had when you was here a spell
back with yore daddy."

"You've seen my dog?"

"Sure did—well, what was left of him. He come
a'dragging in here some days back, more dead than
alive. . . ."

"My dog's *alive?*"

"Was the last time I seen him."

"Where is he? I want to see him!"

"That's what I'm a'trying to tell you, Son. That there pore old mutt come in here busted up something awful. I took keer of him as best's I could. Coming along right nice too, but then this afternoon he got on his legs—real shaky like—and then he took off. Ain't heard hide nor hair of him since, though I took Tug and we went a'looking for him until near sundown."

D.J. turned to Paul and exclaimed, "My dog's alive, Paul! He's alive!"

When D.J. and Paul left the hermit's place with Tug on a chain, the boy's heart was singing with happiness. The big man cautioned D.J. not to get his hopes too high, but the boy couldn't help himself. They made camp well back up from the river in case it rose during the night. D.J. could barely eat his dried fruit and jerky because of his excitement.

Paul moved one end of a dry limb deeper into the camp fire. "Remember, your dog was still mighty weak when he took off from the hermit's place. If he was a'heading home, he's got a powerful distance to go, plus dangers from the land, the weather, and other animals. He might not make it, even yet."

D.J. shook his head vigorously. "He'll make it! And maybe he's not heading home! Maybe he heard us calling and went looking for us. Maybe he's close enough now he can hear us. I'm going to try calling him again."

He finished his last piece of jerky and cupped his hands to his mouth. "Here, Zero—uh—Hero! Here, Boy! Come on!"

The mountain echoes mocked the boy, hurling back his call into the thickening darkness of night. But

even though D.J. listened so hard he seemed to hear
his own heart beating, there was no answering, joyous
bark. At last, weary but still hopeful, D.J., in his tin
pants and coat, curled up by the fire and slept.

* * * * *

Paul was feeding the hounds when the boy
opened his eyes. The eastern sky was paling and the
stars were almost gone above the high rim of the
steep, forested granite canyon where they'd camped.
D.J. started to say good morning, but stopped. The
giant was peering across the river into the dense forests
that clung to the steep hillside. Paul Stagg stood with
his head cocked to catch some sound on the mountain
breeze.

D.J. stood and listened too. It only took him a second to guess the truth. "That's Mr. Abst's and Nails'
hounds we're hearing!"

"From the way they're baying, they've got ol' Mr.
Bear lined out already. Chase is hot; coming this way,
right toward the river. If that's Ol' Satchel Foot—
which is the only bear they'll run—they're chasing one
of the smartest ones I ever heard tell about. Likely
he'll try some tricks when he gets to the river."

"Tricks?"

"Water's the best chance that bear's got, D.J. He's
a'heading straight for it. I'd guess Ol' Mr. Satchel Foot
will use this river to help lose his scent. It's shallow
enough here below the trap that he can wade the river.
Maybe cross and recross it to confuse them even
more. In fact, I got a notion that's what he's been doing
on all those chases he's had recently. Dogs can't follow scent in water, you know."

"That's hopeful," D.J. admitted, "but what chance

do we have that he'll go for *our* trap?"

"The hounds a'jumping him so early like this, that bear may not have had time to have himself any breakfast. So if he confuses the hounds at the river, he's likely to move off a piece and try to grab something to eat. And the easiest thing around is waiting right there for him in our trap!"

"You think he might really do that?"

"He might, 'specially if he gets a whiff of that food we put out for him. Well, we'd best get ready. If that bear comes a'smoking through here and loses Mr. Abst's dogs—as I'm purty sure will happen—then it'll be our turn at Ol' Mr. Satchel Foot."

"What about our hounds?"

"We're probably going to have our hands full holding their muzzles so they can't bark and scare him off. But we won't loosen them unless we have to."

"Couldn't we take the hounds back up wind so they can't smell him?"

"They'll hear the other dogs anyway. Well, let's get breakfast over with so we'll be ready if we get the chance."

By the time the sun had climbed above the eastern canyon rim, D.J. and Paul had heard the Abst hounds make several "loses." But they had sorted out the trail again, judging from the sound. Paul smiled at D.J.

"Well, guess they got that bear 'lined out' again, but they're sure not a'looking at him! He's getting closer and closer. And if he can make this water, Ol' Mr. Bear is plumb likely to get clean away from them again!"

Suddenly, D.J. heard the hounds' baying change. He said anxiously, "It sounds as if they're baying 'treed.' "

The big man cocked his head to listen. "Sure does, D.J. But that can't be! Not two minutes ago those hounds were lining him, but they sure weren't looking at him!"

"Well," D.J. said after listening again, "that sounds like a bear and dog fight to me."

"Can't see how that could be, but that's sure what it is, right enough."

"You mean they've got our bear treed?"

"Don't rightly see how it happened, but that's sure what those hounds are telling the world. Well, we'll soon know because the hunters will come to those dogs."

The boy didn't know how long it was before he heard a heavy rifle explode down the canyon. The sound bounced around the granite-wall like a thunderclap. The sound passed D.J. and Paul Stagg before fading into silence toward Jawbone Peak.

D.J. looked anxiously up. "Think they got him?"

Before the big man could answer, a second shot rang in the distance. When the sound also faded up the canyon, D.J. saw the look of concern on Paul Stagg's face.

"Two shots," D.J. said softly. "Making sure the bear's dead?"

"He's dead, right enough."

D.J. asked, "How can you tell?"

"Listen to those hounds. Different sound to them now. Hear it?"

D.J. listened, aware there was a difference in the trail hounds' tone. He looked up at the big man for an explanation.

"When the gun goes off, a good hound figures the bear is dead. So the hound rushes in expecting to grab the bear's carcass and worry it some. Makes the dogs feel good. Sort of a reward for winning the chase. And the sound Abst's hounds are making now says that's exactly what they're a'doing."

D.J. slowly sank to a stump of a lightning-shattered sugar pine.* "You mean they've killed Ol' Satchel Foot?"

"Can't rightly figure out how it happened, but that sure seems to be the case. Well, there's only one way to make sure. Let's go see."

D.J. shook his head. "I don't feel much like it. I'll wait here."

"I know you're disappointed, D.J., but there's nothing can be done. I want to see how bad that bear's jaw was hurt to make him turn stock-killer. Sure you don't want to come along?"

D.J. slowly shook his head. "That means we've lost the bounty money Dad needed. Kathy'll be hurt when she learns the bear was shot."

"How about you, D.J.? How do you feel?"

"Me? Sort of sick inside. You go ahead. I'll just ease up and take a look at our trap. Maybe some varmint sprung it or stole the bait. You meet me there. All right?"

"Fair enough," Paul Stagg agreed. "But in case that trap does have something else caught in it—like another bear or a mountain lion or anything—you stay back until I catch up with you. Keep that there bush gun of mine handy as an emergency backup, but don't shoot anything unless you have to. OK?"

"OK," D.J. said listlessly. He hoisted the short-

barreled rifle Paul Stagg had loaned him. Back in his
bear hunting days, the big man had explained, he'd
cut the barrel down to legal limits. The standard is-
sue long-barreled Krag was too awkward to carry in
rough country because the weapon was always getting caught in brush.

D.J. double-checked to make sure the hounds
were well tied and out of sight in a little shaded ravine.
The dogs were eager to join the other hounds which
they could clearly hear, but Paul Stagg had firmly
made them be quiet. Paul headed down to the river
to find a place to wade across. D.J. started up the river
toward the trap. His feet moved heavily, feeling like
his heart. Everything had gone wrong—except for one
thing: his little dog probably was alive. But would
the hair-puller ever get out of this deep canyon in his
weakened condition?

When D.J. was about 100 yards from the trap, he
eased up behind a young sugar pine and peered carefully around it. The trap's twin doors were still
standing high above both ends of the heavy metal culvert. The boy glanced down at the river. It was the
most beautiful blue-green where it widened and
slowed across the shallows. There'd be big rainbow
trout in there, the boy knew. Ordinarily, the idea of
fishing for such beauties would have excited D.J.,
but now he just didn't feel much, one way or another.

Out of the corner of his eye, he caught a movement on the far bank of the river. D.J. focused on the
brush which swayed heavily. Something mighty big
was coming through there toward the water. Instinc-
tively, D.J. froze against the rough bark of the tree.

In a moment, a bear's muzzle poked through the

brush and stopped, testing the wind. But D.J. had no doubt. The sight of that deformed lower jaw told the boy that Ol' Satchel Foot was alive! The boy couldn't explain about the two shots and the sound of Abst's dogs worrying a carcass, but it sure wasn't the outlaw bear they'd shot!

D.J.'s heart leaped into a full racing rhythm as the bear moved free of the bush, walked heavily across the water-smoothed rocks. Ol' Satchel Foot plunged into the shallows and waded into the river. The outlaw bear was every bit as big as the boy remembered from their first encounter in the moonlight. D.J. guessed the bear weighed about 300 pounds. If he had not been sick, the animal might have weighed even more.

D.J. wet his forefinger and held it to the wind. It was coming down the canyon from the bear to the boy. D.J. nodded to himself. *Good!* That meant the bear couldn't smell the boy. If D.J. didn't move, the bear's poor eyesight would certainly keep the animal from spotting him.

But what should he do?

D.J.'s mind spun with possibilities. The bear was close enough to the trap he might smell the bait and go to it. Or he might smell the strawberry jam which had been spread around the area and follow that to the culvert. But would the outlaw enter the trap?

D.J. thought about going back for the hounds. But what good would that do? If they were turned loose, they'd take off after the bear, and he'd probably run into rough country, away from the trap.

The boy watched the outlaw crawl out of the river and shake the water off himself like a dog. Suddenly, the big animal stopped and raised his head. D.J. could see him testing the wind. The bear stood on his hind legs like a man. The bear's long neck extended to its limit. The swollen muzzle turned up, the nose sniffing loudly. Then the bear turned toward D.J. and woofed softly.

Quickly, the boy again wet his forefinger and held it up. His heart plunged through his boots. The wind had shifted from him to the bear!

D.J. looked back to the bear. He was gone!

Instantly, the boy knew that the outlaw was now stalking him! D.J. clutched his rifle and looked around for a safe place. The closest was in the branches of the young tree above him.

Ordinarily, D.J. would never have risked the danger of climbing with a rifle. But he knew there was no cartridge in the chamber, and he was careful. Still, it was awkward climbing with the weapon. Fear made D.J. successful. He made it to the first limb about eight feet above the ground. D.J. started to settle on the limb and lean against the trunk. His boot slipped and the boy automatically grabbed for the limb with his free hand. But he jerked the other hand, accidentally hitting the side-loading Krag's cartridge magazine sharply against the limb. The shells popped out.

"Oh, no!" D.J. whispered as all the cartridges fell in bright little brass streaks to the ground. The rifle was totally useless!

A growl jerked D.J.'s eyes away from the precious shells. The outlaw bear was barely 20 feet away, heading straight for D.J.'s tree! The way the bear was huffing and clicking his teeth, D.J. knew the outlaw was mad! And he could climb a tree easily!

In a moment, the bear reached both powerful forepaws around the tree trunk. He opened his mouth wide and began climbing toward D.J.!

Chapter Twelve

DANGER AT THE MAD-RIVER TRAP

D.J. was so scared his mouth was dry as dust. He glanced down as the bear's long hooked claws moved higher up the tree. D.J. drew up his cork-soled boots as far as he could. At the same time, he held onto the empty rifle with one hand and the tree limb with the other. The boy tried to yell, but his voice wouldn't work. Besides, Paul was too far away to help.

The outlaw's coarse black hide hung loosely on his body, like a little boy wearing his father's winter overcoat. The bear's swollen right lower jaw was the size of a cantaloupe. D.J. could see why the bear had turned outlaw and mean. He had apparently been hit by a small caliber rifle bullet which was now infected with "meat bees." These blood suckers looked like yellow jackets. The pain must have been maddening.

As the bear climbed the tree, his yellow tusks clicked viciously. He stretched out his long neck, bringing the open jaws closer to the boy's feet. The tusks closed over the boot heel. D.J.'s voice suddenly returned. He cried, "O Lord! Help me, please!"

He hadn't planned on that prayer, but he meant it with everything in him.

Suddenly, D.J.'s foot was free. Fearfully, he glanced down. The heel had been twisted sideways, but there was no blood. "Thanks!" he whispered, his eyes flickering down to the bear.

His head was tipped back, his nostrils quivering. Whatever he smelled brought a terrible rumbling growl to his chest. As D.J. watched, the bear scooted backward down the tree trunk. Silently as a passing shadow, he padded into the brush and disappeared.

D.J. let his breath out and readjusted himself on the limb. The bear might come back. The boy looked at the shiny shells in the brown pine needles below him.

I've got to have those shells before he comes back! D.J. thought. He glanced around. There was no sign of the bear or any other living thing. D.J. started down for the shells. Then he stopped and turned his eyes toward the sky.

"I'm sorry, Lord," he said softly. "Really sorry. I doubted You when Mom died. But I won't doubt any more."

D.J.'s words stopped, but his thoughts leaped ahead.

Somehow it didn't seem as if he'd said enough. Then he remembered what Paul Stagg had said. Things aren't always what they seem. Man looks on the outside, but God looks on the heart. In that instant, the boy was sure that the Lord was looking at his heart and knew he meant every word. Everything spiritual in him had changed in that moment of time.

A new thought struck him. What had the bear smelled? The hounds, tied with their chains beyond the hill? Maybe Paul Stagg returning? The boy's eyes darted around the area.

He saw the granite cliffs, the river, the steep canyon walls thick with conifers, and shadows from trees retreating before the morning sun. D.J. heard the river gurgling as it rushed over stones. He listened to the breeze whispering in the treetops.

Then he heard another sound. D.J.'s head swiveled toward the bear trap.

Nails Abst was just putting on his pants after having waded the river. The 14-year-old boy had placed his socks, boots, and rifle on a stone beside him. He reached for one sock, keeping his eyes turned up the river bank to the culvert trap.

D.J. started to yell a warning, but it was too late. The outlaw bear exploded from the brush about a hundred feet from Nails. The bear's viciously clicking tusks and short huffing sounds made Nails look around. When he saw the charging bear, Nails didn't reach for his boots or his rifle. He let out a squall and backed up, desperately looking for some kind of safety.

From his tree, D.J. yelled, "The trap! Run into the trap and hit the trigger!"

Nails' eyes darted around, trying to locate D.J. But Nails' glance immediately returned to the bear rushing upon him.

D.J. realized Nails didn't understand that if he ran into the culvert and hit the trigger, both ends would drop down. The heavy iron bars would keep the bear out just as they would have kept him in.

"O Lord! Show me what to do!"

D.J.'s words had barely exploded into the air before he was acting. He wasn't conscious of thinking. He simply held on tight to the rifle, swung his feet well out from the limb, and jumped.

He landed hard, his knees buckling. But he kept the rifle up so the barrel wouldn't fill with dirt and possibly explode when he fired it. D.J. snatched up one glistening brass shell from the pine needles. In one fast movement, he slid the cartridge into the chamber and slammed the bolt home. At the same time, he leaped to his feet and threw the short-barreled weapon to his shoulder. He didn't have his feet well braced as he aimed at the ground a few feet in front of the charging bear.

D.J. didn't want to kill the bear. He just wanted to turn him away from Nails. D.J. held his breath and squeezed the trigger. Since he wasn't well braced, the weapon's recoil* knocked the boy backward. He fell in the dry, brown pine needles under his tree. Instantly, he sat up, fearfully looking toward Nails. He was just getting to his feet after having fallen over a bush.

D.J. also saw something else: the outlaw bear had turned from Nails and was charging straight at D.J.!

He scrambled onto his hands and knees, desperately looking for the rifle. He saw it at once and snatched it up, lifting it cleanly so dirt wouldn't get in the weapon. D.J. started to grab for another shell. But out of the corner of his eye he saw that he couldn't even risk that time. The bear was almost upon him. The boy dropped the rifle and leaped up the same tree trunk he'd climbed a few minutes before. He grabbed the first limb with both hands just as the bear's forepaw struck the bottom of his left foot.

"O Lord!" The prayer exploded from D.J.'s lips as the force of the bear's blow broke D.J.'s grip with his left hand. His body swung out and down. His right palm was torn by the rough bark, but D.J. desperately clung to the limb with that hand. He tried to swing his feet back to the tree trunk to relieve the weight on his one bleeding hand, but it was too late. The bear's forepaw struck again at D.J.'s dangling feet.

But the blow never landed.

A single sharp bark sounded like a small caliber rifle going off. D.J.'s eyes flashed down. Then his throat nearly burst with a glad cry: "Hero!"

The little hair-pulling bear dog was racing from the edge of the forest toward the bear. A string of wild, furious barking poured from the dog's mouth. D.J. saw fresh scars on the rib area. The dog was so skinny he looked like sticks in a gunny sack.

But the dog's brown eyes were aflame with excitement. His voice was strong and sharp, and it was obvious he was threatening to eat that bear all up. The outlaw dropped from the tree trunk and charged toward the oncoming dog, huffing and clicking his tusks.

D.J. swung his feet against the tree, braced himself enough to catch the limb with his right hand. He hung from both hands and yelled, "No, Hero! No! Run! Run!"

The little dog didn't seem to hear him. Dog and bear charged toward each other like a tricycle about to collide head-on with a freight train.

For a moment, D.J. watched the terrible scene. Then he saw the little dog stagger from weakness. The boy released both hands, landed hard in the pine needles and scrambled for rifle and shells.

D.J. raised his eyes as the two animals seemed certain to smash into each other. But the little dog was now bear-wise. He skidded to a halt, sitting so far backward that he slid on the brown pine needles. Then the dog jumped sideways as the outlaw tried to stop.

But the bear's great weight and his momentum wouldn't let him halt. The outlaw's rush carried him past the little dog. Instantly, as the bear passed, the hair-puller leaped up. With a ferocious growl, the dog grabbed a mouthful of bearskin near the short tail and held on.

The outlaw roared with pain and swung around, but the little dog had bounced away like a soap bubble. Barking joyously, his whole body vibrant with life, the dog raced off. The bear chased him with clicking tusks and loud *uf! uf! uf!* sounds.

D.J. snatched up the rifle, but a glance showed him dry pine needles and dirt had fouled both the barrel and chamber. The gun probably would explode if fired. It would take time to clean it. D.J. dropped the weapon again and ran toward Nails Abst while calling to the dog.

"No, Hero! Run! Get away!"

The bear roared and turned his great head back along his body, huge jaws open to crush the dog. But he let go his hold and zipped away, barking furiously. The bear followed him toward the river.

D.J. turned to Nails. The older boy was sitting up,

shaking his head groggily. A small gash on the back
of his head was bleeding freely. D.J. leaped down beside Nails.

"How bad are you hurt?"

Nails felt the back of his head. "Hurts like thunder
where I fell. But I've been hurt worse than this lots of
times."

"Then come on!" D.J. snapped, leaping to his feet.
"That bear'll be back! I've got to help my dog, but
we've got to get you to safety first!"

The mountain boy took a quick look. Bear and
dog were out of sight in the brush, but D.J. could hear
the little hair-puller's sharp, loud barks. D.J. could
also hear his hounds. Apparently, they'd either smelled
or heard the bear. D.J. knew they'd be trying to
break their chains and join the fight. But D.J. couldn't
depend on that. Hero was now on his own.

Nails was tottering uncertainly on his bare feet.
"Where we going?"

"Into that trap! Come on!"

"You crazy? I'm not going in *there!*"

"It's our only chance. Here, let me help you. Put
your arm over my shoulder and run with me. And
when we get there, you bend over and scoot in that
near end! I'll take the other end!"

"I told you, I'm not going—"

D.J. interrupted. "You want that bear to get you?
Then do as I tell you! Be careful, though! When you get
inside, don't touch the trigger until I tell you."

D.J. helped the older boy crawl into the open end
of the culvert. "Now just sit there!" D.J. ordered, starting to run alongside the galvanized trap. "Don't you
touch anything! You hear?"

In a moment, D.J. had reached the other open end of the culvert and slid inside. "Thanks, Lord!" he breathed and sucked in his breath to call out. "Here Hero! Here, Boy!" D.J. tried to whistle, but his mouth was so dry from fear he couldn't pucker right.

Nails exclaimed, "Oh, now I get it! We hit the trigger and both ends close so the bear can't get us! My dad will hear the shot and come. . . . I'll hit the trigger."

"No!" D.J.'s voice was so sharp the older boy jerked his hand back. "No!" D.J. repeated. "We've got to wait until my dog gets here too!"

"You crazy? That bear'll be right behind him!"

"I'm not going to let that bear get my dog! Don't touch that trigger!"

D.J. cupped his hands and called the hair-puller again. It was like yelling in a barrel. But the little dog heard. He burst from some brush and streaked for the trap.

But the hair-puller was too weak from his recent wounds. He was slowing, staggering, about to fall. D.J. knew the bear would come bursting through the brush in a minute.

D.J. leaped out of the safety of the culvert trap and ran forward. Just as the bear smashed through the brush, D.J. held out both hands to the tired little dog. "Jump! Jump!"

With a happy, weak voice, the hair-puller obeyed. D.J. caught him and spun around. He ran hard, trying not to fall, and hearing the outlaw gaining with every step. Still holding the dog in his arms, D.J. dived headfirst through the open end of the trap.

"Now, Nails! Now!"

Nails raised his foot and kicked the smelly trigger hard. That released the gates on both ends of the trap. The heavy iron bars smashed down with a loud clang!

D.J. crushed the happy little hair-puller to his chest and swung around just as the outlaw bear slammed hard into the bars, inches from D.J.

For one terrible second, D.J. thought the bars weren't going to hold. Then the bear bounced back and let out a squall of pain and frustration.

D.J. hugged the little dog that was happily licking his face with a slurping tongue.

"Oh, Hero! You'll never know how glad I am to see you!"

The outlaw tried every way possible to get into the trap. He reached ugly, hooked claws through the iron bars. The boys drew themselves up tight in the center out of reach. In a little while, they heard Abst and Paul Stagg shouting. In a few moments, the men ran into the opening on the opposite riverbank. D.J. saw both men throw their heavy rifles to their shoulders.

D.J. yelled, "Don't shoot! We're safe inside the trap!"

The men lowered their weapons. Paul called, "You both in there?"

"With my dog! We're safe! Don't shoot!"

Tinsley Abst yelled, "But the bear'll get away!"

"Let him go!" D.J. yelled through the bars. The culvert echoed with a hollow sound. "His life for ours! Please?"

Nails pressed his face against the bars at the near end of the trap closest to the river. "The bear's going! Leave him be, Pa! Leave him be and come get us out of here!"

D.J. held his breath as the professional hunter again lifted his heavy rifle to his shoulder. The barrel followed the outlaw bear bounding uphill for cover. D.J. saw Paul Stagg's big hand reach out and push the rifle away. D.J. heard the big man's booming voice.

"I think two boys' lives for one bear's is more than a fair exchange."

Tinsley Abst lowered his weapon. "Guess you're right. OK, let's get across this river and free those boys!"

* * * * *

Before noon the next morning, D.J. rode in the front seat of Paul Stagg's borrowed pickup. It ground in low gear, climbing slowly up the logging road from Devil's Slide Canyon. The little hair-puller was sleeping, weak, exhausted but happy, on the floor-board. Hero's muzzle rested on the boy's boots. D.J. turned to look at the hounds and Zeke Zeering's borrowed turn-in dog. They rode in a box on the back of the pickup. They hadn't been needed.

D.J. lifted his eyes to the culvert trap secured on the trailer which bounced behind the pickup. Both iron barred doors were down and locked on the trap. Through the nearest barred door, the boy saw Ol' Satchel Foot riding in the trap.

The driver chuckled. "D.J., yesterday afternoon it sure didn't look like we'd catch that outlaw. Yet there he is."

"If he was a regular bear, we still wouldn't have him, either. I'm sure glad you figured he might come back last night and had us reset the trap."

"Well, he's not afraid of people. I thought he

might hurt so much from that sore jaw that he'd risk coming back to where he'd smelled that bait yesterday afternoon. Probably figured it was easy food like he's been getting around man."

"Kathy'll be glad to know we'll have a vet treat that sore jaw. When he's well, maybe Kathy can ride with us when we take Ol' Satchel Foot up to the high country and let him loose."

"I'm sure she'd love that, David." The lay preacher looked in the side rearview mirror at the captured bear. "That ol' bear came within an inch of having things turn out different. Yesterday Abst and his son were gaining on Ol' Satchel Foot when his hounds ran smack-dab into that sow. Plain accident, her crossing that outlaw's trail when it was so hot. But the Absts had to shoot her to save their hounds. That gave Ol' Satchel Foot a chance to escape."

"And scare me and Nails half to death! But at least he and I had a place to hide from that bear! But you'd been in real trouble if you'd run into him in the brush while going to see about those two shots we heard."

Paul Stagg nodded. "If it hadn't been for all that, you'd have lost the reward money, for the Absts would have taken that outlaw for sure."

The boy turned to look at the driver. "That sure was mighty nice of Mr. Abst to say he didn't have any claim to the bounty on that bear."

"It's all yours, D.J.! Sorta Mr. Abst's way of saying 'thanks' for saving his son's life."

"I still think you should take half! After all, it was your idea to reset the trap and camp nearby last night."

"Just a hunch I had, D.J. Not worth any money to

me."

"Well, thanks again, then. And I'm thankful God answered my prayers in that tree."

"He always hears prayers we mean, D.J."

The boy felt good inside. "You were sure right awhile back when you said things aren't always what they seem. We thought Zero—I mean—Hero, was afraid of bears. But he wasn't; I guess he changed."

"He was afraid, but he changed because he loved you more than his own life, D.J."

"And Grandpa changed because he made his commitment to Jesus. And He changed me back there in that tree. Do you think there'll be singing and laughter in our house again, like before Mom died?"

"I'm sure of it, D.J. And we'll keep on praying for your father too. My wife and daughter are praying for him, and I know Mrs. Higgins is praying too."

The boy was thoughtful a moment, then he thought of something else. "Is there any chance we can stop and see where the Absts had to shoot that mother bear? If she had a cub hidden in a tree, it'd be mighty hungry by now."

The giant's rumbling laughter erupted from his big chest. "I didn't see any sign of a cub, but we'll take a look anyway. Say, what would you do if there *was* one?"

"Take it home. Raise it like you did your cub."

"D.J., I doubt your dad would let you have a cub. Especially now that you're going to keep that hair-pulling bear dog. But we'll stop, just to make sure."

"Thanks."

"D.J., there's something I been meaning to tell you. Last night I was praying about leaving Stoney

Ridge for Sheet Iron Mountain. A Bible verse came to mind. Even stayed with me in my sleep. Was still there when I awoke to the sound of Ol' Satchel Foot tripping that trap. Been too busy to talk about it until now."

"What verse was that?"

"It's from Jeremiah 42:10 where God says, 'If you will indeed stay in this land, then I will build you up and not tear you down, and I will plant you and not uproot you.' "

D.J. swallowed hard. "Does that mean you don't have to move away?"

"It means I'll help get Sheet Iron Mountain's church going again, then I'll be back. Kathy will go to school here and I'll get to see all you young people grow up strong in the Lord."

D.J. let out a happy yell. Hero raised his head and looked at D.J. who bent to pat him. "Hey! Now that I've got my dog back, I can hardly wait to see what's going to happen next!"

The big man laughed. "Me too, D.J.! Me too!"

* * * * *

D.J. didn't know it, but his next exciting adventure would start in a few more minutes. Just what happened to D.J., his family, and friends—and especially the hair-pulling dog and an unexpected new pet—is told in the next exciting D.J. Dillon adventure book,

The City Bear's Adventures

LIFE IN STONEY RIDGE

BLOODHOUND: A breed of dog that has a keen sense of smell. A hound's sensitive nose enables it to detect both foot scent on the ground and body scent brushed off on grass and bushes. Trained bloodhounds can usually follow a trail that is several hours old. Some can follow older trails if the scent is not destroyed by other scents or by rain or snow. The bloodhound has a very wrinkled face and long, droopy ears. His coat is usually tawny, or black and tan, or red and tan.

BULL PINE: Another name for a ponderosa pine. Because of unfavorable growing conditions, a bull pine usually doesn't stand more than 75 feet tall. A bull pine has hard, dark bark with deep furrows.

CHOKE-SETTER: A lumberman who prepares downed trees for the heavy equipment that will take the trees out of the woods. The choke-setter digs a hole or tunnel under the downed tree trunk. Then he throws a strong steel cable over the log and pulls it back through the hole. He puts the knob on one end of the cable through a loop on the other end and pulls the cable tight around the log. A tread-type tractor then hooks onto the log and pulls it out of the woods.

CONIFERS: Another name for the many cone-bearing evergreen trees or shrubs. Spruce, fir, and pine trees are all conifers.

CRACKLINGS: A dog food made of pork scraps or trimmings that have been heated and pressed to get rid of most of the fat.

CRICK: Another word for creek.

FEIST: A small mongrel dog.

HACKLES: The hair on a dog's neck and back that stands up when the dog is angry or afraid.

HAIR-PULLER: A small, quick dog of mixed breed. A hair-puller's natural tendency is to go for the heels or backside of any animal, including sheep, cows, or bears.

HEELER: Another name for a hair-puller or "cut-across" dog.

IRISH SHILLELAGH (pronounced "Shuh-**LAY**-Lee"): A cudgel or short, thick stick often used for a

walking cane. A shillelagh is usually made of black-
thorn saplings or oak and is named after the Irish vil-
lage of Shillelagh.

KRAG: An old military rifle with a very long barrel
and a side-loading cartridge chamber.

MONOLITH: A very large, single block of stone.

PONDEROSAS: Large North American trees used
for lumber. Ponderosa pines usually grow in the
mountain regions of the West and can reach heights
of 200 feet. The ponderosa pine is the state tree of
Montana.

RECOIL: The sudden jerk or kickback of a gun
upon firing.

SHOATS: Another name for young, weaned pigs.

16 HANDS: This term refers to the way of measur-
ing a horse's height. A "hand" equals 4 inches, the av-
erage width of a man's hand. Horsemen measure the
height of a horse from the ground to the highest point
of the withers (the ridge between a horse's shoulder
bones). Any full-grown horse standing 14.2 hands (14
hands and 2 inches) or less is called a pony. Most
racing and riding horses stand 15 to 16.2 hands high.

SPRINGFIELD OUGHT SIX: An Army rifle that
was issued in 1906.

SUGAR PINE: The largest of the pine trees. A sugar

pine can grow as tall as 240 feet. Its cones range from 10 to 26 inches long and are often used for decoration.

D.J. DILLON
• ADVENTURE SERIES •

The Hair-Pulling Bear Dog
D.J.'s ugly mutt gets a chance to prove his courage.

The Bear Cub Disaster
When his pet bear causes trouble in Stoney Ridge, D.J. realizes he can't keep the cub forever.

Dooger, The Grasshopper Hound
D.J. and his buddy Alfred rely on an untrained hound to save Alfred's little brother from a forest fire.

The Ghost Dog of Stoney Ridge
D.J. and Alfred find out what's polluting the mountain lakes — and end up solving the ghost dog mystery.

Mad Dog of Lobo Mountain
D.J. struggles to save his dog's life and learns a hard lesson about responsibility.

The Legend of the White Raccoon
Is the white raccoon real or only a phantom? As D.J. tries to find out, he stumbles upon a dangerous secret.

The Mystery of the Black Hole Mine
D.J. battles "gold" fever, and learns an eye-opening lesson about his own selfishness and greed.

Ghost of the Moaning Mansion

Will D.J. and Alfred get scared away from the moaning mansion before they find the "real" ghost?

The Secret of Mad River

D.J.'s dog is an innocent victim — and so is the hermit of Mad River. Can D.J. prove the hermit's innocence before it's too late?

Escape Down the Raging Rapids

D.J.'s life depends on reaching a doctor soon, but forest fires and the dangerous raging rapids of Mad River stand in his way.

*Look for these exciting stories
at your local Christian bookstore.*